1992 Merry Christmas!
To: Amanda
From: Mom &
Dad

JOURNEY to TEREZOR

P9-ELR-672

Frank Asch

BULLSEYE BOOKS • ALFRED A. KNOPF
NEW YORK

1) Silver Pyramid

Matt Hilton lay on his bed playing a game of Space Warp on his new minicomputer. For the most part his concentration was so complete that the rest of the world ceased to exist. But every now and then he became aware of his parents talking in the next room.

"Let's face it, you've never enjoyed our annual camping trips." Mr. Hilton closed the lid of his fishing tackle box. "I'm not surprised you're ready to throw in the towel just because of a little rain."

"A little rain! I'd hardly call four solid days of constant downpour a little rain." Mrs. Hilton turned up the radio and poured herself another cup of coffee, her third since breakfast.

"Flooding in the eastern portions of the state have resulted in extensive property damage but no casualties have been reported . . . *whirrrrrrrrrr, sssssssss* . . . While the rain is expected to continue . . . *ffffffffff* . . . *sssssss* . . . state authorities are now warning all vacationers in the Monroe wilderness area to evacuate at once . . ."

In less than twenty minutes the Hiltons were packed and ready to go.

"As soon as we cross the Monroe Bridge we'll be on high ground." Mr. Hilton slowed the family station wagon to steer around a branch that was lying in the road.

In the backseat Matt peered out the rain-streaked window. "And what if the Monroe Bridge is washed out, Dad? Then what do we do?"

"Just like your mother," grumbled Mr. Hilton. "If worries were nickels, you'd both be millionaires."

Matt shrugged his shoulders and began yet another game of Space Warp.

Screeeech! Mr. Hilton jammed on his brakes. Ahead, the road was completely washed out. Minutes earlier, the river had swept away any trace of the Monroe Bridge.

"I wanted to leave yesterday, but no, you had to wait just one more day! Now what are we supposed to do?" complained Mrs. Hilton.

Mr. Hilton considered getting out of the car to see if there might be some way to ford the stream. But as he reached for the door handle, a giant oak fell across the road with a loud *womp!* "I guess we have to go back to the cottage," he said meekly.

The rain was coming down so hard it was difficult to see the road ahead even with the wipers going full speed.

"I've driven through much heavier rain than this," said Mr. Hilton, his chest pressed against the steering wheel. "Don't worry, we're going to be just fine."

Matt turned off his minicomputer and slipped it into the custom-made secret pocket of his jacket. *I don't think Dad realizes how serious this is.*

The rain was coming down harder than ever. As they drove, the ditches swelled, overflowed, and reached across the roadbed. By the time they returned to the cottage, the waterline was up to the foundation.

"What about the Glenborough Dam?" said Mrs. Hilton as she closed the front door behind her.

"What about the Glenborough Dam?" grumbled Mr. Hilton.

"I just read an article last week that said it was long overdue for repairs. If it breaks we're going to need a submarine to get out of this valley."

"I never saw that article!" snapped Mr. Hilton.

"Look, Dad, water's starting to come through the cracks in the floor. What do you say we tie up the furniture and make some kind of raft?" suggested Matt.

Mr. Hilton looked at his son as if he had suggested they should sprout wings and fly. "Nonsense, it won't get that bad. We'll just go upstairs and wait."

"Wait for what?" said Mrs. Hilton. "Noah, to come by in his ark?"

"Wait for the rain to stop." Mr. Hilton took his wife by the hand and started up the stairs.

Before they had taken two steps a loud *thwack!* resounded through the air. The heavy timbers of the cottage screeched as a wall of cold brown water pushed in the windows like a wrecking ball. In a matter of seconds three feet of water covered the entire first floor.

"The Glenborough Dam must have burst! Quick! Upstairs!" cried Mr. Hilton.

At the top of the stairs Mrs. Hilton reached out and pulled Matt close to her. "Don't worry, Matt, we're going to be all right." She stroked the tiny beads of muddy water from his thick brown hair.

Peering through the spokes of the banister, Matt watched the old-style wooden houses of the family Monopoly game float down the hall and into his bedroom.

Mr. Hilton was the first one to hear the helicopter. "Listen! They're coming for us!" he cried. At first the whirring of its blades was very faint, hardly distinguishable from the sound of the rain. But it soon grew louder.

Mr. Hilton threw open the window and grabbed a pillow from the bed. Allowing the pillow to fall into the muddy water beneath the window, he waved the pillowcase like a flag of surrender.

The helicopter seemed to know they were there. It was heading straight for the cottage, dropping a rescue line as it hovered nearer.

"This way! Follow me!" Mr. Hilton climbed out the window onto the porch roof. Matt followed, then Mrs. Hilton climbed through.

They could see neither pilot nor crew but a powerful loudspeaker from within the open bay of the craft boomed down instructions: "Hold on to the bars and slide your feet into the metal rings."

The rain was still falling hard. As Matt reached up to grab hold of the rescue line, rain pelted his face.

"Hold on tight!" cried Mr. Hilton.

With a smooth efficiency the helicopter winch

hauled them inside and the loudspeaker dictated additional instructions: "Stand clear of the open bay. Take one of the seats in the rear of the passenger cabin and buckle your safety belt."

"That was a close one," said Mr. Hilton as he took a seat next to Matt.

The bay door to the helicopter had closed automatically and warm air was flowing into the cabin. The air helped to lessen the chill of wet clothes but it also made everyone feel sleepy.

"Look down there!" cried Matt. "The cottage is starting to float downstream!"

"What?" Mr. Hilton strained to hear Matt over the roar of the helicopter engine.

"The cottage!" hollered Matt. "It's floating away!"

Any minute, Mr. Hilton expected the copilot or one of the crew to come down to the passenger cabin to check on them. When no one did, he concluded that the crew must be preoccupied, locating other victims of the flood.

"We're flying above the clouds. Isn't that unusual for a helicopter?" asked Matt.

"What?" hollered Mr. Hilton.

"Never mind," said Matt.

Mrs. Hilton leaned her head on her husband's shoulder and allowed her eyelids to lower.

Mr. Hilton yawned and closed his eyes. It didn't

make sense that they should be so suddenly and overwhelmingly sleepy. Mr. Hilton considered the possibility that they were being drugged, but quickly dismissed the thought.

In a few moments Mr. and Mrs. Hilton fell into a deep sleep.

Matt also felt sleepy, but something out the window caught his attention. Yawning, Matt rubbed his eyes and looked again. No, it wasn't possible, but there it was. About a hundred yards from the helicopter, hanging in the sky like some gigantic Christmas tree ornament, was a huge silver pyramid!

"Mom! Dad!" Matt called to his parents but they did not answer. "Wake up!" he yelled and shook them to no avail.

Losing the battle to stay awake, Matt watched a rectangular door at the base of the pyramid slide open while the helicopter engine went dead. The blades above Matt's head coasted to a stop, but instead of falling, the helicopter hovered in midair like a tiny feather floating in a gentle updraft. Then slowly it drifted toward the open door of the enormous silver pyramid.

2) Earth Pouch

When Matt woke up, he was lying next to his mother and father on a fold-out couch in a strange living room. His mother was sleeping soundly. His father was snoring. Matt sat up, rubbed his eyes, and yawned.

"Hi."

Startled, Matt whipped around. A very thin boy with chalky white skin and stringy, jet black hair was sitting on the far side of the couch.

"Who are you?" asked Matt.

"Ryan Morrison," said the boy in a nasal voice. "The arrival shelter was full so they brought you here."

The shades were drawn, but a beam of light from

the window's edge struck the wall above the couch, illuminating a satellite photograph of Earth.

"Where am I?" Matt sat up and swung his feet into his shoes. He had a terrible headache, and his ears were ringing.

"You're in our living room. My parents aren't home right now. My mother's at the Community Center helping to put on a play. My father's a doctor. He's at the infirmary. He told me to call him when you woke up." Ryan took a pen from his pocket, pushed a button on the clip and spoke into it: "792405 . . ."

"Yes, Ryan. Are they up yet?" The full-bodied voice of Dr. Morrison emerged from the pen.

"Just the boy," said Ryan. "The mother and father are still sleeping."

"Give him some water to drink and take him for a walk; it will help with his headache and the ringing in his ears," said Ryan's father. "I'll be home as soon as I'm finished here."

"Okay, Dad. Should I tell him?"

"Sure, go ahead. Talk to you later. I'm busy now."

Ryan switched off the pen.

"That's some gadget you have there," said Matt. "May I see it?"

Ryan handed the pen to Matt.

"It's called a remote," said Ryan.

"Hmm, no brand name. Must be Japanese," said Matt.

As Matt examined the pen he wondered how Ryan's father knew about his headache and the ringing in his ears. Then he remembered the Silver Pyramid. *Must have been a dream.*

"How long have I been asleep?" asked Matt.

"At least twelve hours," replied Ryan.

"What did your father want you to tell me?"

Ryan stood up. "Come on in the kitchen. I'll get you a drink of water. What's your name?"

The kitchen was very high tech. The ceiling and floor both glowed with an even yellow light, while the chairs around the kitchen table and the table itself seemed to float in midair.

Looks like a set for a science fiction movie, thought Matt.

"I've never been the one to tell anybody before," Ryan spoke hesitantly as he handed Matt the glass of water.

Matt drank the water and smiled. "Tell me what? That I'm on another planet?"

Ryan looked shocked. "How did you *know*?"

"Know what?" asked Matt.

"That you're on another planet."

Just then there was a knock at the door. "Anyone home?"

"Come on in, door's open," called Ryan.

It was Sara Hollings who lived next door. Sara was about the same age as Matt and Ryan. She had a pretty face with large green eyes and a turned-up nose. Her hair was bright red and long, but she wore it pushed back in a single braid. Sara's movements were quick but graceful, and her voice had a musical lilt to it. Even though she was wearing ordinary jeans and a simple T-shirt, something about her reminded Matt of a pixie or a wood nymph.

"Hi, Ryan." Sarah looked past Ryan to Matt. "You must be the new kid from Earth."

From Earth? Matt wondered if he had heard Sara correctly.

As soon as Ryan introduced Sara to Matt, she started firing questions at him.

"Where are you from?" she asked.

"I'm from Ohio, but we just moved to the suburbs of New Jersey," replied Matt, wondering if the throb in his head was ever going to go away.

"Suburbs . . . that's not quite country and not quite city," said Sara, wanting to show that she knew what the word suburbs meant, "and New

Jersey . . . that's next to New York. I bet you go to a lot of shopping malls. Did you ever see the Statue of Liberty?"

"Don't mind her," said Ryan in response to Matt's puzzled expression, "she was born here."

"Born where?" asked Matt anxiously, remembering the Silver Pyramid again. "You don't actually expect me to believe I'm on another planet, do you?"

"You mean he doesn't know yet?" asked Sara.

"No, I just told him a second ago," said Ryan.

"Oh, I'm sorry," said Sara.

"If this is your idea of a joke, I don't think it's very funny," said Matt. "Now tell me where I am . . . really!"

"You're at Earth Colony on a planet called S-15," said Ryan.

Normally Matt liked practical jokes, and he didn't mind being kidded now and then, but this was ridiculous.

"Look, my family and I were in a serious flood," said Matt. "We almost got killed. So it's really not a good time to joke around. *Where am I?*"

Ryan knew how it felt to be in Matt's position and he didn't want to say the wrong thing.

"I can still remember five years ago when this happened to me. I was just seven years old. My parents and I were flying back from Europe. The captain told us to fasten our seat belts. All of a sudden there was a big explosion, and we woke up here, same as you."

"Except for people born here, like me," said Sara, "everyone at Earth Colony has a similar story to tell. Some were caught in fires, others got lost in the wilderness or their boat sank. Anytime there's an accident on Earth and the bodies aren't recovered, chances are they end up here."

Matt laughed nervously. "You've been reading too many *National Stars.*"

"*National Stars?*" said Sara.

"You know, the newspaper they sell at the checkout counter in all the supermarkets: PYGMY GIVES BIRTH TO BIG FOOT. ALIEN RACCOONS INVADE UTAH."

"Supermarkets?" said Sara.

"You better let me handle this, Sara." Ryan poured himself a glass of water and took a sip. As always, Ryan's movements were slow and deliberate.

He drinks a glass of water as if he were diffusing a time bomb, observed Matt.

"At first I thought my parents were just teasing me about being on another planet," said Ryan. "I thought we were in some kind of theme park. . . ."

Only half listening to what Ryan was saying, Matt walked over to the window, pushed back the curtains, and looked out.

"Houses, grass, trees, sky, looks kind of like Earth to me, guys!" Matt smiled confidently.

"Maybe we ought to take him out to the dome," said Sara. "That usually convinces people."

"Excellent idea!" Ryan turned to Matt. "We'll take you by the new construction site. Probably you'll be living in one of the houses they're building there. Dad said I should take you for a walk, anyway."

"The dome? What's that?" asked Matt.

"The dome is the magnetic force field that surrounds all of Earth Colony," said Sara as she opened the kitchen door. "It's transparent, so you can see what S-15 really looks like."

"Is that so?" At this point Matt was convinced that someone in Ryan's family was an inventor or a futuristic kitchen designer, and he was dealing with two dedicated practical jokers. For the time being, at least, he decided to play along with the gag. "Tell me now, what does S-15 really look like?"

"Green sand," said Sara. "Nothing but green sand as far as the eye can see. No rocks, trees, or anything else, just green sand."

As Matt stepped outside, he noticed some mud

from the flood was still caked on his shoe. He rubbed his heel against the step, knocking the mud to the ground.

"Wait a minute." Ryan bent down and scooped up the claylike soil in his hand. "I'll be right back."

"Where's he going?" Matt asked Sara.

"Up to his room to put that soil in his nature collection."

"But it's just ordinary dirt, why on Earth would he want to save it?" asked Matt.

"That's just it," answered Sara, "we're not on Earth anymore."

"Oh yes, I almost forgot. We're on another planet," said Matt with a singsong voice and a big wink.

"You can make a joke out of it if you want to," said Sara, "but everything green that you see here is growing in synthetic soil. I wouldn't mind having a piece of Earth myself."

"Do you have a nature collection too?" Matt knocked his shoe against the step, and several more clumps of soil fell off.

"No, but I just made an Earth pouch, and I've been wondering what to put in it." Sara bent down and very carefully picked up the small particles of soil.

"An Earth pouch? How interesting. What's an

Earth pouch?" said Matt, thinking to himself: *She's either a very good actress or a complete nut case!*

"You wear it around your neck. It's kind of like a good-luck charm. Lots of kids, especially the ones born here, have them. They fill them with things that remind them of where they really came from. Everyone wants to get a stone from Earth. Any kind of stone. But they're hard to come by. One kid I know has an acorn in his. I guess it's kind of like a fad. But I don't care." Sara withdrew a tightly woven cloth pouch that was hanging from a string around her neck. She opened the pouch and poured in the soil from Matt's shoe.

3) Invisible Wall

"Okay, I'm ready now." Ryan came out the front door and slowly walked down the steps one at a time.

Gosh, he walks like an old man, thought Matt.

"Thanks for the soil, Matt." Ryan was genuinely grateful. "If you ever want it back, let me know. I'm going to analyze it and look for microorganisms. There may even be a seed in it. If there is, I'll attempt to grow it."

"I doubt I'll want it back," said Matt, as they left Ryan's yard and set out down the street.

"You may change your mind," said Ryan. "After you've been here for a time, you really get to appreciate anything that comes from Earth. But this planet is fairly interesting too. I've been conducting a small archaeological dig just outside of town. We'll pass it on the way to the dome. Except for a few fossils, I haven't found much so far: early life-forms, seashells, things like that. Whatever life S-15 once supported, it seems to have died off early on."

For a while they walked along in silence. As far as Matt could tell, everything looked perfectly normal. It was like walking through a middle-class housing development. Most of the houses were made of white stucco with neatly trimmed lawns and white picket fences. But slowly, Matt began to notice small discrepancies. For example, none of the houses had chimneys or mailboxes.

"There are no clouds here," said Sara, "but it rains every Tuesday and Thursday. It rains for exactly thirty-seven minutes and then stops. There used to be lightning and thunder, but lots of the older folks complained about all the noise so the orbs don't bother with it now. I've never seen clouds, myself."

"Orbs?" said Matt.

"Yes, there's one now." Ryan pointed to a metallic sphere that was floating down the street. The sphere was about eighteen inches in diameter and looked like a giant, shiny bead of mercury. As it approached, hovering about four feet above the ground, Matt watched his own warped reflection in its highly polished silver surface grow larger.

"Good morning," said the spherical robot.

Stunned, Matt stared at his own shrinking reflection as the sphere passed by and continued on down the street.

So far Matt had been able to dismiss everything he saw as merely unusual, but the sight of the orb totally unnerved him. "That thing, that *orb* was levitating! And the voice was so human! What *was* that thing?"

"That's one of our hosts," said Ryan, deriving a subtle but distinct pleasure from Matt's astonishment. Ryan's initial assessment of Matt was that he was a rather simple-minded, boring kind of person. *Perhaps he's intelligent*, thought Ryan, *but he's not very intellectual. Clever but not really smart. I doubt that we'll become friends.*

"You mean it's alive?" asked Matt.

"No, it's a robot," said Sara. "There're dozens of them here on Earth Colony. They run the whole place."

Once again Matt remembered the Silver Pyramid. Its gleaming silvery surface was exactly the same as the orbs. *Maybe it wasn't a dream after all.*

"If it's a robot, then someone has to have made it," said Matt.

"The orbs say they were created by an advanced race from the planet Terezor. But no one here has ever seen a Terezor and the orbs won't even tell us what they look like," said Sara.

"Why would orbs snatch people from Earth and bring them here?" asked Matt.

"They say they want to preserve the human species in case something happens to Earth: nuclear war, greenhouse effect, whatever. They say there are lots of colonies here on S-15, all of them from endangered planets like Earth," said Sara.

Could Ryan and Sara be telling the truth? thought Matt. *Everything they're saying is so bizarre.*

"I still don't believe you, but let's say you are telling the truth. When do we get to go home?" asked Matt.

"Home? Back to Earth? Never," sighed Sara. "We're prisoners here like mice in a cage. Unless . . ." She let her voice trail off mysteriously.

"This is just too weird," said Matt.

"You want to know what's really weird? Most people end up liking it here!" said Sara with disgust. "There's hardly any crime or serious disease," explained Ryan . "Work is optional. The orbs take care of everything, from providing food to picking up the garbage. People like that. They like the golf course and the amusement park and holovision. That's three-dimensional TV."

By now they had come upon the construction site. It was about a city block wide. Foundations for several housing units were already in place, and a team of orbs were raising walls.

For Matt, watching the orbs at work was like witnessing a magic act. Without the use of arms or hands they levitated their laser saws and vacuum hammers in an intricate ballet that was both graceful and highly efficient.

"I've never seen anything like that. I don't think anybody has!" gasped Matt. Matt was totally transfixed. Without taking his eyes off the orbs, he reached into his secret pocket and pulled out a pack of gum. Unwrapping a stick for himself, he offered the pack to Ryan and Sara.

"No thanks, but I'd like the wrapper," said Ryan.

"The wrapper? Do you collect gum wrappers too?"

"No, he just needs the aluminum foil for a circuit board. Ryan's building a homemade computer," said Sara. "I'll chew the gum."

"Why don't you just buy a computer?" Matt asked Ryan as he handed Sara the gum.

"They're a forbidden item around here. In fact,

I'd appreciate it if you didn't mention to anyone what Sara just told you." Ryan cast a withering glance in Sara's direction as he spoke. "The orbs are very touchy about computers."

"Well, you can borrow mine anytime you want." Matt reached into his secret pocket and pulled out his minicomputer. "It's just a handheld but . . ."

"Can I? . . . Is that really? . . ." Sara snatched the computer out of Matt's hands as if it were the brass ring on a merry-go-round.

"It was a birthday gift from my grandfather. He's an engineer," said Matt. "He said it does lots of stuff, but I just use it to play video games. I'm really tops at Space Warp."

"Look, Ryan, it's not just a calculator," exclaimed Sara. "It's a computer!" Though she had never seen a computer before, Sara's highly analytical mind quickly grasped how to handle its various functions. As she watched the numbers fly up on the view screen, she felt as if someone had tied a helium balloon to her spirit and sent it soaring high above the town.

"Come on, there're too many orbs around here." Ryan hustled Sara away from the building site.

"Guess you've never had your own computer," said Matt as he followed Ryan and Sara down the street.

"It's not just that!" exclaimed Sara. "Except for the orbs themselves, there *are* no computers on Earth Colony. The orbs usually confiscate them. It's a miracle yours got through."

"Must be my secret pocket," said Matt. "Ever since I was a little kid, I've had my mom sew one into the lining of my jackets."

"May I see?" asked Ryan.

Sara handed Ryan the computer.

"Will it quantify quadratic factors?" asked Ryan.

"Sure. It will even handle Fourier transformations," exclaimed Sara.

"How about set integers?"

"Up to the nth power. Now we can compute integration and derivatives."

"Sounds like you guys are really into math," said Matt.

"The orbs run the schools here," said Ryan. "They don't tell you much about themselves or how their technology works, but they're *great* math teachers."

"You see, I knew it would happen!" exclaimed Sara.

"You knew what would happen?" asked Matt, noticing that the ringing in his ears was now only half as loud and his headache was beginning to fade.

"That somehow we'd get a computer. Now I can

compute the missing variables and try out my formula," said Sara.

"What kind of formula?" asked Matt.

Sara turned to Ryan and he shook his head. "Let's just say we want to reprogram something."

Matt felt like someone trying to put together an endless puzzle. Every time he got a piece to fit, a hundred more pieces got dumped into his lap.

As they walked along, Sara and Ryan kept passing Matt's computer back and forth. To Matt it seemed like every other word from their mouths was a number. At one point Matt considered showing them how to play Space Warp, but quickly decided against it.

Ryan and Sara were so absorbed in their own conversation that without intending to, they ignored Matt. But Matt was too awed by their obviously superior intellect to be offended. *These kids must be geniuses! Real whiz kids!*

Matt was feeling much better now. The ringing in his ears was almost all gone and so was the headache. It felt good to be walking. Matt let himself relax and put the orbs and everything Ryan and Sara had said about being on another planet out of his mind. After a while the houses thinned out and the road ended abruptly in the middle of a wheat field.

"This way." Sara led Matt around the yellow sea

of ripening grain into a forest of evenly planted pine trees.

For several minutes they walked through the shady forest. While Ryan and Sara spouted numbers and formulas and pushed buttons, Matt enjoyed the fresh air and pleasant fragrance of pine. Then suddenly the forest stopped.

"We're here!" Sara stood still and let herself fall forward. Matt was just about to reach out and catch her when she held out her hands and stopped. Poised in midair at a precarious forty-five-degree angle, Sara smiled. "This is the dome."

Matt extended his hand. For a few inches the air seemed to thicken. Then it became very dense. Moving his hand forward, he felt a weak electric current tingle in his fingertips. Finally the air in front of him became a wall, solid, invisible, and hard as steel.

Beyond the wall as far as he could see lay a desert of green sand.

4) New Life

"On another planet! I can't be on another planet! It's impossible! I've never even been to another country! Things like that just don't happen to ordinary people from the Midwest!" exclaimed Mr. Hilton.

Even when Matt took his father out to see the dome, Mr. Hilton refused to face facts.

"There must be some logical explanation for all this," he muttered to himself as he put his hands up against the invisible wall. "I'm having a nervous breakdown. That's it! The strain of the flood must have pushed me over the edge."

Unable to explain his experience any other way, Mr. Hilton concluded that Earth Colony was really a mental institution and the orbs were doctors and nurses.

"Though I admit I'm hallucinating and I see you as a floating, talking sphere," Matt heard his father say to an orb in the street one day, "another part of me knows that's absolutely impossible, and I just want to say that you can count on me to cooperate fully with my rehabilitation."

Mrs. Hilton's first reaction was pure hysteria. In fact, she got so upset Ryan's father had to give her a sedative to calm her down. By the time the sedative wore off, however, she succeeded in reasserting her usual self-control.

It took a crew of five orbs only three days to build the Hiltons' new house. But Mrs. Hilton refused to move in until they repainted the walls with colors to suit her taste. She also had them redo the curtains and put in thicker carpeting.

The day the Hiltons moved, the neighbors gave them a housewarming party. One by one, people arrived with special dishes of hors d'oeuvres, casseroles, and desserts.

"Pleased to make your acquaintance." Mr. Hilton acted the perfect host as he greeted them at the door. But to himself he muttered, "They say they're my new neighbors, but I know better. Today must be visiting day at the hospital."

It was pretty scary for Matt to see his father acting so strangely.

"What are we going to do about Dad?" he kept asking his mother.

"Just give him time," replied Mrs. Hilton. "I know your father. Once he's made up his mind about something, nothing we say or do will change it. But you'll see. He'll come around on his own."

Mrs. Hilton's assessment proved to be one hundred percent correct. One night, about a week after they moved into the new house, Mr. Hilton broke down and started to cry. He was sitting on the couch watching holovision when all of a sudden he slowly lowered his head into his hands and sobbed.

"It's true, it's true, we really are on another planet."

Mrs. Hilton put her arm around his shoulder and held him. In about twenty minutes it was all over. He got up, went outside, and cut the lawn.

After that, Mr. Hilton seemed to adopt Mrs. Hilton's no-nonsense attitude.

Even Matt was surprised to see how quickly his mother adapted to their new life. In a few days she had made friends with the neighbors, joined the women's auxiliary, taken up sewing, and become a member of the gardening club. She seemed to thrive in the new environment.

"What with the autowash and the menu oven, this house practically runs itself," she boasted to Mr. Hilton one afternoon over a cup of synthetic coffee, "and now that you don't have to work, we can spend lots of time together like we always wanted to."

Mr. Hilton had some trouble getting used to the idea of not having a job to go to. But after he joined the bowling league and the fly-casting club, he too was on his way to complete adjustment.

The orbs had furnished Matt's room with all kinds of neat toys. There was a remote-control submarine, a self-propelled kite, a rubber ball that would bounce all day, a mechanical dog that was hard to distinguish from a real one, and a host of other gadgets and construction toys more elaborate and interesting than anything Matt had ever seen.

Matt's favorite new toy was his portabike. The portabike looked like an ordinary bicycle, until Matt pushed a certain button behind the seat. Then it collapsed into a rectangular cube, small enough to fit into a backpack. The thing Matt liked best about the portabike was that it was so light. Riding it was like pedaling air.

Almost every day after breakfast Matt got on his portabike and went for a long ride. Earth Colony was over thirty miles in diameter, so there was a great deal to explore. Matt spent the first week just cruising the downtown area, walking through the shops and service centers. Most of the shops were run by orbs, but sometimes people took them on as hobbies. There were clothes stores and furniture shops and every kind of commercial establishment that you would find in an ordinary town. The orbs gave out money credits every month and people could buy as much as they wanted, whether they worked or not.

Matt's favorite store was called The Sweet Shoppe. The orbs insisted that everything sold in The Sweet Shoppe, mostly ice cream and candy, was not only harmless to the teeth but just as nutritious as vegetables and protein. Matt never failed to stop there for lunch.

Another favorite stop on Matt's rounds was Luna Park. Luna Park was an amusement park designed and run by the orbs. It lay just outside of town, between the reservoir and African animal reserve. It had all the usual rides that any amusement park had: a Ferris wheel, a roller coaster, bumper cars, and so on. But they were much bigger and wilder. The roller coaster, for example, went ten times higher and faster than the one on Coney Island. In addition to going up and down it did loop-the-loops and spun around like a cement mixer. And most amazingly, the orbs designed all the rides so the passengers never got sick to their stomachs.

In addition to the conventional rides, the orbs added a few designs of their own. Of these, Matt's favorite was called The Smasher. It consisted of a huge cranelike apparatus mounted on a circular track. The passengers were seated in a large wrecking ball which dangled from the top of the crane. As the crane rolled around on the track, the ball with the passengers inside swung back and forth, smashing into walls of magnetic bricks. Matt loved the sensation of crashing through the walls and watching the bricks fly every which way. He also liked the way the orbs were able to make the magnetic bricks fly back into position at the end of each ride.

Matt made friends easily, and there were plenty of kids his age in the neighborhood. On Earth, Matt used to play shortstop in the Little League. He was quick, batted well, hardly ever made an error, and had an arm that could peg the ball into the first baseman's glove with a sting. Earth Colony had two teams in Matt's League: the Asteroids and the Orbits. Matt could have gotten on either team, but he picked the Orbits because he thought they needed him more.

The first day he tried out for the team he got to play shortstop in spite of the fact that the Orbits already had one. Matt was so good, even the old shortstop didn't resent being replaced with a new kid.

Although Matt had all the right stuff to be popular, he preferred to keep to himself. Whenever other kids invited him to play he politely refused. After a while they stopped asking. Even when he helped the Orbits win an important game, he went for a ride all by himself on his portabike instead of going to The Sweet Shoppe with the rest of the team to celebrate with malts and ice-cream sundaes.

Of all the kids on Earth Colony there were only two that interested Matt: Ryan Morrison and Sara Hollings. They were so grown up and scientific; not at all like any of Matt's former friends. In fact, whenever he was around them, he didn't quite know how to act or what to say. Matt didn't know why, or even what it was about Ryan and Sara that so strongly attracted him, but more than anything, he wanted to be their friend.

Sara seemed to like him well enough, but Ryan, though never rude, tended to be aloof and sometimes downright cold. Matt didn't take it personally; Ryan and Sara didn't seem to have time for *anyone*. They were always together, working in Ryan's workshop or Sara's room with the door closed. Whenever Matt went over to visit and asked to play, they politely refused.

5) Level Seven

"Now remember," cautioned Ryan, as they waited on a quiet street for an orb to come by, "we've only had Matt's computer for a little while. It may take weeks more before we're really ready to reprogram."

"I'm not so sure about that," said Sara as she took the two alligator clips from Matt's computer and attached them to the transphaser, an orb device Ryan had "borrowed" from his father's medical bag. "According to my calculations we have more than enough transfer relays to multisequence the necessary data bursts."

"But for all we know, orbs are booby-trapped. One false move and it blows up in our face," argued Ryan.

"You worry too much," said Sara.

"You don't worry enough!" countered Ryan. "We stop at level three, or I'm quitting right now."

Reluctantly, Sara agreed. "Okay, we'll stop at level three, if we ever find an orb, that is. Seems to me we've been waiting for an awful long time. Any other day we would have seen five of them by now."

"They're probably at the hydroponic plant," said Ryan. "I heard they're installing a new filtration system this week."

"Hi, guys," Matt greeted Ryan and Sara as he rode up on his portabike, "mind if I hang out with you two for a while?"

"Actually we're kind of busy right now." Ryan lowered his voice. "We're testing Sara's formula today."

"Oh, yes, my computer." Matt pushed the button on his portabike that automatically made it collapse into a small rectangular package. "I was kind of wondering if I could borrow it back sometime to play Space Warp. I haven't played a single game since I got here. I'd hate to lose my knack."

As soon as the words were out of his mouth, Matt thought to himself: *What a stupid thing to say! What they're doing with my computer is probably a heck of a lot more important than my silly video game.*

"As soon as we're done here, you can have it for the evening," said Ryan.

"How's it been going?" asked Sara.

"Well, not too bad." Matt tried his best to sound casual as he sat down on his collapsed portabike. "I guess I was pretty homesick for the first week, but I'm okay now."

"Miss all your friends?" asked Sara.

"I'd just moved from Ohio so I hadn't had time to make any new friends in New Jersey."

"Ohio, that's where they grow all the potatoes, isn't it?" asked Sara.

"No, that's Idaho," said Matt.

Just then a bullet floated past and parked halfway down the block. Bullets were the car-sized, bullet-shaped vehicles the orbs used to haul small cargo. Like the orbs, they levitated about four feet above the ground on a cushion of antigravity.

The bullet hovered for a moment, then its hatch popped open and an orb emerged.

"Here we go!" While Ryan monitored frequency levels, Sara turned on the computer and started feeding her formula into the makeshift relay transmitter.

Suddenly the orb began to bob up and down even as it moved forward.

"Fantastic! We've already penetrated descrambler defenses!" cried Ryan. "Try a lateral adjustment, and ease into level two."

Sara continued to work the buttons on the computer.

Suddenly it dawned on Matt what Ryan and Sara were doing. "I don't believe it. You guys are reprogramming an orb!"

"Good. Now insert integral formulations, and I'll adjust frequency," cried Ryan.

Sara pushed more buttons.

"Excellent! Now level three!"

Sara continued to operate the computer, and the orb began to wobble.

"Incredible!" gasped Matt. "You're controlling it!"

"Not controlling, not yet, just affecting," said Ryan. "We could go further, but we're going to stop here . . . for now, at least."

Sara was thinking about how wonderful things would be, once they were free of the orb's authority. They would be able to do anything and go anywhere, even to Earth, *especially* to Earth. And it was all in the palm of her hand!

"Watch this!" Sara punched another series of keys on the computer.

"No, don't!" Ryan reached out and tried to grab the computer.

"It's okay." Sara pulled away and continued to push buttons. The transmitter was vibrating with a low hum and the red overload light was blinking wildly.

The orb stopped moving forward and began to spin slowly on its vertical axis. Then it made a high-pitched whine and shot out a pink laser.

"Oh no! I wasn't expecting that!" Sara mumbled to herself.

"You idiot!" cried Ryan. "Give me that thing!"

Turning slowly, the orb's laser sliced into the first object it encountered. A tree across the street was severed in two. Then a streetlamp fell. All the while the laser kept moving steadily toward the house on the corner.

"Cancel! Cancel!" cried Ryan.

"Can't! Got to go all the way now!" Sara proceeded to push buttons, her fingers flying over the keyboard.

Just as the orb's laser reached the house, the deadly pink beam switched off and the orb fell to the ground.

"Phew! That was lucky!" exclaimed Sara.

"Lucky! I think we've done it!" cried Ryan.

"You mean! . . ."

"Yes," said Ryan, "knocked out primary functions and penetrated the program core to level seven!"

"You know, I think you're right!" Sara looked dazed as she and Ryan walked toward the fallen orb. "Gosh! I didn't think it would be this easy."

"Easy!" exclaimed Ryan. "I nearly had a heart attack! Key in verbal control so we can get out of here before another orb comes along."

Ever since the orb cut down the tree and the lamppost, Matt had been standing with his mouth hanging wide open. "I knew you guys were smart"—he stood up and walked over to the fallen orb—"but this! This is fantastic!"

"I think I've got it now." Sara pushed a few more keys on the computer. "Activate levitation."

As soon as she spoke, the orb rose off the ground.

"Good, secondary memory is still intact." Sara addressed herself to the orb. "We are Sara, Ryan, and Matt and your name is . . ." She stopped. "Quick, we need a name!"

"Call it Cyber," said Ryan.

"Okay," Sara continued, "your name is Cyber, and we are your masters. Maintaining our safety and following our instructions are your primary objectives. Is that understood?"

"Yes, Sara," said the newly reprogrammed robot, "and may I inform you . . ."

"What's your specialty?" asked Ryan.

"I'm a matrix module, seven fifty-nine," said Cyber, "and may I inform you . . ."

"Matrix module? What's that?" asked Matt.

"Cyber's what they call a drifter," said Ryan. "He floats through the system assisting whenever extra help is needed."

"May I inform you that at this very moment you are all in grave danger," said Cyber, raising his speaking voice double its normal volume. **"As soon as you took control of my primary program core, a separate but parallel circuitry began to broadcast an alarm."**

"Oh no! That's just the kind of thing I was afraid of!" cried Ryan.

"What kind of alarm?" asked Matt.

"Cyber is equipped with a security system. It's kind of like a burglar alarm. Apparently, it has already gone off," cried Ryan.

"But I don't hear a thing," said Matt.

"It's a radio alarm!"

"That's correct, Ryan," said Cyber in the same tone of voice he'd use if he were officiating at a spelling bee or helping an old lady across the street. "It's entirely reasonable to assume that other orbs are on their way here at this very moment. They are programmed to view you as a highly threatening hostile force and will deal with you accordingly. I could put a force field around you and attempt to protect you with my lasers, but I am afraid we would be hopelessly outnumbered. Unless we proceed quickly upon a judicious course of action, we will all be subject to termination."

"Termination?" Matt looked up and down the street, expecting at any moment to see an orb careening around the corner, firing its lasers.

"The course of greatest possible safety is disassociation," continued Cyber. "That is, I suggest you all make a run for it!"

"And you won't tell it was us who reprogrammed you?" asked Ryan.

"In keeping with maintaining your safety, the first of your major commands, I will self-destruct prior to revealing that information," said Cyber.

"Okay, that's good enough for me! Come on. Let's get out of here!" said Ryan. He took Sara by the hand and started to run.

"Wait a minute!" Matt stepped up to the orb. "Cyber, let's say we didn't run. Is there anything else we could do?"

"There is an alternative course of action, but I don't recommend it," replied Cyber.

"I didn't ask for your recommendation," said Matt. "Just tell me what you have in mind."

"Do you have a remote?" asked Cyber.

Matt reached into his pocket and took out his pen-shaped remote.

"Yes," he said.

"It has a minimemory chip," explained Cyber. "If you come with me in my bullet and turn it on and off as I instruct you, I *might* be able to use that memory to turn off my own alarm."

"It's no good," Ryan called to Matt. "Sara and I will try again when we're better prepared. Come on!"

Matt longed to be more than just the kid who happened to bring Ryan and Sara a computer. He wanted to be part of their team.

"You guys make a run for it. I'll stick with Cyber."

"No, Matt, it's too dangerous!" begged Sara.

"No problem, I'll just go for a little ride with Cyber and be right back," said Matt as he ran over to the parked bullet.

"Don't do it!" cried Sara.

"Come on, Cyber." Matt commanded the orb to get into the bullet and climbed in after it. His body was tingling with anticipation, his senses were on edge. He felt totally present, a concentrated form of his usual self.

"Let's go!" he cried.

6) New Data

The windowless bullet rode so smoothly that for a
time Matt didn't know they had already departed.

"What's the problem? Why aren't we moving
yet?" asked Matt.

"We are moving," replied Cyber. "Presently we
are traveling at top speed toward Earth Colony's
force field dome."

"It's dark in here. Can't you turn on a light or
something?"

"Pardon my error," said Cyber, and instantly a
white light above Matt's head came on. "Are you
quite comfortable?" The interior of the bullet was a
hollow compartment with no padding or seats.

Kneeling on the floor Matt could raise his hand and almost touch the ceiling.

"Yeah, I'm comfortable enough, but don't worry about that. Think about turning off the alarm!"

"Rest assured my thinking processes operate simultaneously on several different levels. At this very moment I am computing alternative solutions to the alarm assignment. Please turn your remote to the On position and push the button marked Record."

Now that Matt was alone with Cyber he began to feel a little less daring. *This won't take long,* he reassured himself. *With any luck, Cyber will turn off the alarm and we'll be able to sneak back into Earth Colony in a matter of minutes.*

"Where are we now?" Matt asked Cyber.

"We just went through Earth Colony's force field dome."

"But I didn't feel a thing."

"There's nothing to feel. This vehicle is equipped with a counter force field shield."

"Are we being followed?"

"Radar report: negative. But there are courier bullets with expressmode drive. This kind of vehicle could easily overtake us. It's only a matter of time before one is set on our trail. We must endeavor to keep our spirits up. Think positive thoughts. That will raise your morale and increase your chances of success and survival. Would you like me to play you some music?"

"Skip the music," said Matt. "Just kill that alarm!"

"Please set your remote to the Off position," replied Cyber. "I am sorry to report that it is impossible for me to turn off the alarm."

"But I thought you said . . ."

"I said I could not guarantee . . ."

"But you haven't worked on it for more than a couple of minutes!" Matt was angry.

"I could repeat my calculations any number of additional times, but I am absolutely sure the results would be the same. If I proceed any further, it's almost one hundred percent certain that I'll trigger my self-destruct program."

Time to cut my losses, thought Matt.

"Take me back to Earth Colony," he instructed Cyber.

"That option is no longer available," reported Cyber. "In all likelihood we would be fired upon before we got through the dome."

"Won't the bullet protect us?"

"Laser shielding is not standard equipment for this category of vehicle," replied Cyber.

Matt had wrongly assumed that as long as he was

inside the bullet he was safe. *You can still handle this situation,* he told himself. *Take it easy. Don't panic. That will only make things worse.*

Suddenly Cyber announced: "New data: Radar shows that we are being tracked. An expressmode bullet is rapidly closing in on us. Recommendation: We alter our present course and proceed toward the nearest dome: Galator Colony. Request permission to act upon recommendation."

Cyber spoke faster than usual, so fast that Matt had to strain to understand him.

"Okay, go ahead." Matt's sense of being on a grand mission no longer gave him courage; all his bravado was gone. His thoughts were like a roomful of jumping rabbits going nowhere. *This was stupid. Am I going to die now? There must be some solution. Think fast. Think about what? You're stuck. Maybe you should just tell Cyber to stop and get out. No. That's crazy. Or is it? You're just a kid. They wouldn't kill an unarmed kid. Would they?*

"Permission acknowledged, initiating course change now. Proposed plan of action: As soon as I drop you off I'll turn around and set a head-on collision course with the bullet that's chasing us. Just before impact, I'll abandon ship. If all goes well, they'll assume that you and I were destroyed in the crash. I have my own counter force field shield which will enable me to penetrate the dome of Galator Colony and rejoin you within a few minutes of the crash unless I've been destroyed or captured. If captured, I will self-destruct. In that case you will be on your own."

"On my own! You've got to be kidding!" said Matt.

"I am not programmed to be humorous unless requested," replied Cyber. "Time of arrival at Galator Colony, approximately forty-nine seconds. Listen carefully to the following data. Your survival may depend on it: Galators are what is termed 'full evolutionaries.' The mature Galator is a large, highly intelligent bird that lives in the mountains but lays its eggs as it flies over the sea. The eggs fall into the sea and hatch into fish. The fish, after living in the sea for some time, grow legs and develop lungs. They become amphibians and leave the ocean to live in tidal pools along the beach. There, they continue to develop until they become reptiles. The reptiles, in turn, leave the beach and migrate to the jungle where they grow hair and develop into mammals. The mammals grow into apelike creatures and finally humanoids called Dars. Do you understand?"

"Yeah, I think so," said Matt. "They go through

the entire process of evolution in a single lifetime."

"Correct. When the Dar stage of their development is achieved, they leave the jungle one by one and wander into the plains beyond," continued Cyber. "The physical appearance of individual Dars varies considerably. Some have dark greenish skin, others bluish. A few have skin like yours. Recommendation: Your best strategy for survival, should you be forced to fend for yourself on Galator Colony, is to impersonate a Dar. When they leave the jungle they are hardly more than hairless apes. You'll have no trouble passing yourself off as one."

"Thanks a lot. I appreciate the vote of confidence."

"The Dar or Dars that take you in will treat you well. Their food is safe for you to eat and as long as they think you are one of their own species, they will educate you in their language and customs."

Suddenly the hatch door popped opened.

"Galator Colony?" gasped Matt.

"Affirmative," said the orb.

As Matt leaned forward and looked down he discovered that the bullet was hovering above a large body of purplish water.

He knew he couldn't stay in the bullet, but its hard shell felt so much safer than the strange body of water beneath him.

"Can't you take me to the shore?" he asked.

"No time," replied Cyber, and rotating the bullet with a jerk, he propelled Matt out the hatch door.

Arms and legs kicking, Matt sprawled through the air and entered the purplish water with a splash.

7) Hot Seat

As the bullet disappeared from view, Sara burst into tears.

"It's all my fault! If I hadn't gone to level seven, this never would have happened!"

"Don't be so hard on yourself." Ryan's eyes locked onto Sara's. "We programmed Cyber to follow instructions and guard our safety, right?"

"Yes." Sara tried to look away, but Ryan's eyes were like guided missiles. Once they zeroed in on target, there was no way to shake them loose.

"So Cyber is looking out for Matt," said Ryan. "They have lasers, a bullet, and a head start. They've probably left Earth Colony by now and . . ."

"What about the alarm?" said Sara.

"Cyber will think of something. And if he can't, we will!" Ryan hurried Sara down the street.

"What are you talking about?" Sara took a big gulp of air and forced herself to stop crying.

"We've still got our equipment. We'll program another orb and send it to help Matt."

By this time they were standing in front of Ryan's house.

"W-w-what are we doing here? We have to go to Matt's house and tell his parents."

"No, we can't tell anyone!" insisted Ryan.

"Not even Matt's parents?" asked Sara.

"Especially not Matt's parents! They'd just blame us and take away our reprogramming equipment. Then we couldn't help Matt at all."

"But Matt's parents could go to the orbs and beg them to spare him," argued Sara.

"Matt's parents are bound to be emotional and upset. If they slip, if they mention our names just once, then we're on the hot seat too! You heard what Cyber said: 'They . . . view you as a highly threatening hostile force.' That means they'll shoot first and ask questions later. Matt has Cyber to protect him. But what have we got? Nothing! Matt may survive just fine, but chances are we'd get fried to a crisp because we're the ones with the computer and the transmitter. Think about it, Sara! You've seen what the orb's lasers can do. We'll be reduced to a zero. Zero divided by one multiplied by a billion is still zero!"

Sara knew that Ryan was making good sense. But lying wasn't in her nature. *We have to tell them the truth!*

Just then a bullet shot by. It came up from behind, streaked past in a blur, and was gone in the blink of an eye.

Sara had never seen one travel so fast. "They're after Matt, I know it!"

"You coming or not? We've got work to do." Ryan started walking up the steps to his house.

Sara turned in the opposite direction, toward Matt's house. She took a few steps and stopped. Then she reached into her T-shirt, pulled out her Earth pouch, and squeezed it.

It was 2:20 on a Tuesday, one of the two pre-scheduled times each week when the orbs' climate control mechanisms began to cool the warm moist air of Earth Colony. As Sara turned and followed Ryan into the house, she heard the whisper of artificial raindrops falling on the roof.

8) Purple Water

Matt knew he could tread water for just so long, and he couldn't depend on Cyber coming back to get him. He had to swim to shore and, if necessary, seek out help. He slipped off his shoes and let them sink into the purple water.

Stay calm, keep your wits about you. Remember what Yogi Berra once said: "The game isn't over until it's over." The shore, a beach of green sand, lay approximately one quarter of a mile away. *I've never swum that far before. I'd better take it easy and pace myself. If I get a cramp I'm finished.*

Matt started to pull himself through the water. He could see a lush green jungle beyond the beach and above the jungle the peaks of several craggy, snowcapped mountains.

Suddenly there was a brilliant flash of light. The bullets had collided! Matt spun around in time to catch the tail end of an enormous blaze. It was impossible to estimate how far away the crash had taken place, but from the look of the smoke rising up into the sky, he guessed it was two or three miles beyond the Galator dome.

There goes Cyber. I hope he made it.

With every stroke toward shore, Matt's jacket filled with water, dragging and slowing him down. He slipped his arms out of the sleeves and let it drift slowly downward.

Suddenly, hundreds of little red fish attacked Matt's jacket. Their white teeth glinted up through purple water as they tore the jacket to shreds and devoured everything but the zipper. In a matter of seconds the jacket was gone.

What was that?

Matt felt something grab at his pant leg and yank off a piece.

Oh no! They're after me!

All of a sudden he was surrounded by thousands of hungry little mouths.

They're going to eat me alive!

Matt pictured the little white teeth cutting into his flesh like so many thousands of tiny razor blades, red blood mixing with the purple water.

"Ahhhhhhh!" A scream of terror exploded from his mouth. *Get away from me. No! No! Leave me alone!* Matt thrashed in the water like a tiny animal in the jaws of a great beast.

But the fish would not be discouraged. They circled around like a swarm of monster bees— darting forward, attacking and retreating before Matt could react. Overwhelmed, he squeezed his eyes shut, and let himself go limp. Floating in the water like a piece of debris, jagged thoughts of horror echoed through his mind. *Soon they'll tear out my eyeballs and pick the flesh from my bones!*

But the red fish were only interested in eating Matt's clothes. Never once did they so much as touch his body.

"So you like to eat clothes!" Matt yanked off his underwear for the fish to feast on. "Here, take these too!"

When all of Matt's clothes were devoured and the buttons were seesawing down through the dark water, the school of strange fish simply swam away.

Without the encumbrance of clothes, Matt's body slid through the water with an ease that gave him additional strength. His future was uncertain, but for the moment, he let himself enjoy the sensuous pleasure of swimming naked. It reminded him of the time he and some friends went skinny-dipping in the river behind the school. It was a sweltering summer day, and they had spent the whole morning earning money cutting lawns. Their bodies were hot and sweaty, and their jeans and T-shirts were sticking to their skin like flypaper. The water had been cool and refreshing. It never occurred to the boys that it might be polluted until they saw some dead trout floating downstream. *This purple water may be deadly*, thought Matt. *Whatever else happens, I'd better not drink any.*

When Matt reached the shore, he dragged his body out of the water like a sackful of wet seaweed and collapsed onto the beach of green sand.

Exhausted, he closed his eyes and let himself rest for a moment. Then something moved. Startled, he opened his eyes and saw a large orange frog just inches from his nose. *So you're what the little red fish grow into.* Matt sat up slowly. He thought of catching the frog but decided against it. *It looks harmless enough, but it might be poisonous.*

"Blurrrrp!" The frog leaped straight up into the air and hopped away.

Matt got to his feet and looked around. Small pools of violet water dotted the beach everywhere.

Each pool hosted a dozen or so of the orange frogs. Up the beach near the jungle, large yellow lizards were hiding under twisted logs.

In a different circumstance Matt would have enjoyed exploring the beach, but now he was more concerned with his own survival. Anxiously, he searched the horizon for some sign of the spherical robot. *Cyber said that he would be back in a few minutes. That must have been half an hour ago. With my luck he got blown up in the crash. By now he's probably nothing but a pile of scorched computer chips.*

Time passed slowly. Matt had nothing to do but talk to himself while he waited.

Okay, so I goofed up. What else is new? Everyone makes mistakes. Maybe I didn't succeed as I hoped I would. But I'm still alive. That's something. Something? Heck! It's a lot more than something. It's a miracle! All I need is a few more miracles and everything will be all right. It would be easier with Cyber but who needs that bucket of bolts, anyway? I'll make it on my own!

Matt began to worry about staying warm after sunset. *Maybe I should wait longer, but it's going to get a lot colder when the sun goes down. I'd better find some kind of shelter by then.*

Matt decided to give up on Cyber, and set out through the jungle for the village of the Dars. As he stepped beyond the thin line of scrubby trees at the edge of the beach, the sweet smell of decay filled his nostrils, and the moss underfoot gave way like a spongy carpet.

Some of the trees towering above his head resembled gigantic flowers, others looked like enormous mushrooms. Next to tall palms were doughnut-shaped growths that lay on the ground like old tires. Matt knew he was awake. But the jungle had such an otherworldly quality to it; he felt as if he were stepping into a dream.

About a half hour into the jungle, Matt was standing in a patch of tall purple ferns when he heard a loud shriek. Out of the corner of his eye he caught a glimpse of a bearlike creature rushing past. The bear had reddish fur and very long legs.

That must be what the lizards grow into. He waited a moment to calm down and then continued on.

Gradually, the jungle took on more and more of the appearance of a forest until finally Matt emerged into a partial clearing of brambles and pricker bushes. A structure that resembled a log cabin lay beyond the clearing in a field of tall grasses.

That must belong to a Dar.

Slowly, hesitantly, Matt walked toward the cabin.

When he was just forty feet or so from the door, it opened and a Dar stepped out. The Dar was wearing a gray robe made of a single piece of cloth. He had long purple hair and light blue skin.

This is ridiculous! He'll never accept me as a Dar. I don't look anything like he does.

Gesturing with both hands, the Dar bade Matt to come closer.

Matt's heart was thumping like a screen door banging in the wind. He wanted to turn and run. But there was nowhere to go.

Matt stepped forward. The Dar rapidly blinked his eyes and ran his hands up and down Matt's arms and shoulders. Matt shivered with the strangeness of the creature's touch, but he also found it gentle and friendly.

He accepts me. He thinks I'm a Dar! thought Matt, and he stopped shivering.

At close quarters, Matt could see that the Dar's body, although very similar, was also quite different from his own. This Dar had a wide forehead, bloodshot eyes, yellow lips, and a nose that looked as if it were trying to escape from his face.

Pointing to himself, the Dar said, "Vaata."

"Vaata," repeated Matt. Vaata was very pleased

at the success of his first language lesson. Stepping lightly, he hopped about, dancing in a circle around Matt. Then he stopped suddenly, as if remembering something of great importance, and solemnly led Matt into his cabin.

9) Rock Star

In many ways Vaata's home reminded Matt of an early settler's cabin. Its walls were made of trees cut from the forest, notched and crisscrossed at the corners. Coming up through a layered straw roof was an ordinary-looking rock chimney, but the straw was a bright orange color and inside the cabin, instead of boards or dirt, the floor was covered with the same spongy moss that grew in the jungle.

I'm the first human being to meet a Dar and step inside a Dar household. I guess this moment is kind of historic, like Balboa discovering the Pacific or Armstrong on the Moon. Too bad I don't feel historic, just cold and hungry, thought Matt as he followed Vaata to the back of the cabin toward a wooden chest. The chest was very simple in design, but expertly crafted. Vaata opened the chest, withdrew a large gray cloth, and held it out to Matt. It was a finely woven piece of material, a robe like the one he was wearing.

"Gar beege," said Vaata.

Matt pulled the robe over his shoulders.

"Gar beege." Vaata tied a green sash around Matt's waist and danced around the table and chairs that were in the center of the cabin. Patting the seat of one of the chairs, Vaata bid his guest sit down.

"Gar corrule."

That's easy, thought Matt. *Gar must be the Dar word for you. Gar beege. You wear. Gar corrule. You sit. Beege, wear. Corrule, sit.* Matt was an average student in math and most other subjects, but his school in Ohio had a special language program. For two years running he had gotten straight A's in advanced German. All he had to do was say any new word three times to himself and it was memorized. *Gar beege, Gar beege, Gar beege. Gar corrule, Gar corrule, Gar corrule.*

While Matt watched, Vaata worked at a counter near the door, preparing a meal of chopped Dar vegetables.

"Margeea." Vaata held up a leafy vegetable with fuzzy yellow skin.

"Margeea," repeated Matt.

"Dooa! Dooa!" Vaata blinked his eyes rapidly.

Dooa, I bet that means good, thought Matt.

Matt could hardly believe his eyes when instead of a knife Vaata began to chop the vegetables with his bare hands. The back of Vaata's little finger was as sharp as a kitchen knife. *I'd hate to have a karate fight with this guy!* thought Matt.

While Vaata worked, he hummed joyously to himself, pumping his arms and tapping his feet. When the meal was ready, he could contain himself no longer. He took a plate of food in each hand and danced around the cabin. Leaping and twirling in a most vigorous but graceful fashion, Vaata delivered the two plates to the table without spilling a single morsel of food.

Then Vaata sat down and chanted a prayer. To Matt, the prayer was a collection of meaningless sounds, but in the days that followed, Vaata patiently taught him the meaning of the prayer. It was called:

PRAYER OF WELCOME
Welcome, you who have come from the
    forest,
To learn, to grow, to know,
My hands, my fields, my house,

Let them serve us,
That we may learn, to grow, to know,
The ways of our winged selves
The true people of the mountain.

When Vaata finished, he blinked his eyes rapidly. Sensing that the blinking of eyes was meant as a friendly gesture, Matt blinked back. Matt soon realized that Dars considered the showing of teeth to be a hostile gesture. Instead of smiling they blinked their eyelids. Lost in spasms of ecstasy at Matt's response, Vaata jumped up and began to dance all over again. He flapped his arms, swooped around the table, tumbled head over heels in the moss, and leaped up, touching the ceiling with his fingertips.

I sure picked a strange Dar to take me in. I wonder if they're all like this.

Later Matt discovered Vaata's behavior was quite normal for a Dar. He learned that there were few words of emotional expression in the Dar language. Dars expressed their feelings through sound and movement, through song and dance. Vaata, while expressive and exuberant by human standards, was considered somewhat reserved, almost stoic in personality, compared to most Dars.

But Vaata was not stoic today. To host a newly

emerged Dar, one fresh from the forest, ignorant of Dar ways and customs, was considered an honor above all others.

Vaata picked up some food from his plate with his fingers. Matt did the same. The food looked very strange and smelled like perfume. Matt couldn't remember if Cyber said the food was safe to eat, but he was hungry. *I've got to eat something.*

When Matt picked up one of the yellow leaves from his plate and opened his mouth, Vaata wrinkled his forehead.

"Naagaa," said Vaata disapprovingly.

Matt lowered his hand, and Vaata reached across the table and placed some food near Matt's lips.

Oh no! He wants to feed me! Matt leaned forward and let Vaata put a morsel of food on his tongue. Then Vaata blinked his eyes and opened his mouth. His tongue was bright blue.

And he wants me to feed him! I think I'm going to gag!

Matt placed some food in Vaata's mouth. *It's a good thing I have a strong stomach.*

"Dooa! Dooa!" cried Vaata.

Vaata was overjoyed at how quickly Matt learned the Dar way of communal eating. Once again, he leaped up and began to dance around the room.

What's this guy think he is, a rock star or something?

Sitting down, Vaata started to feed Matt and encouraged Matt to feed him. At first Matt felt extremely awkward. He kept thinking: *Someone from another planet is putting his fingers in my mouth.* But after he got over the initial shock, he relaxed and enjoyed his meal.

Matt found Dar food to be quite flavorful. Some of it was even sweet. The yellow leafy portion of the meal was very much to Matt's liking. The leaves had a strong nutty flavor and a crunchy texture unlike anything Matt had ever tasted before. He also liked the pasty brown substance that Vaata spooned into his mouth. It tasted something like sweet potatoes mixed with maple syrup. *Not as good as eating in The Sweet Shoppe but I guess it will do.*

When dinner was finished, Vaata expressed pleasure with Matt's table manners by performing a jolly little dance with his hands. One by one and together he flexed his fingers and intertwined them in complex patterns and rhythms.

Just as an experiment, Matt did a little dance with his hands too. It was not nearly as graceful or expressive as Vaata's gesturing, but it pleased Vaata no end. Once again, unable to contain his joy, he leaped up onto his chair and danced exuberantly, kicking his feet and bobbing his head as he hummed and sang.

The star around which S-15 revolved had set barely an hour ago, but Matt was exhausted. When Vaata motioned that Matt should lie down on the soft mossy floor, he was more than willing to oblige.

For a while Matt lay there thinking and watching Vaata dance as he cleared off the table.

I wonder how long I'll be here. It might be weeks, months, maybe even longer.

Mom and Dad must think I'm dead. Darn! How was I supposed to know things would end up this way? But I can't think about that! I'm in big trouble, giant, economy-sized, jumbo trouble. I've got to concentrate on staying alive and bide my time until Ryan and Sara reprogram another orb. They're the only ones who can save me now.

Matt pulled the Dar poncho around his neck, and reviewing the Dar words he had learned that evening, fell into an uneasy sleep.

10) Stun Ray

When the orbs informed the Hiltons that Matt had been killed in a bullet collision, they apologized profusely but at the same time blamed Matt for the incident.

"Though we don't know how, your son seems to have stowed away in a bullet and willfully damaged its navigational functions, thus causing the accident," said the orb assigned to the task of dealing with Mr. and Mrs. Hilton.

If it weren't for Ryan, Sara would have told Matt's parents what really happened, but Ryan insisted that they say nothing.

"We've got to keep quiet," he lectured Sara

constantly. "For all we know the orbs captured Matt and killed him."

"Or Cyber could have staged that crash to cover up their escape," said Sara. "So far the orbs haven't said anything about Cyber being reprogrammed. But how could they not know? They must suspect something."

"They know all right," said Ryan. "They just don't want us to know they know. They're smart and they're tricky. That's why we can't let down our guard. From now on we have to be more careful than ever."

Ryan and Sara worked in utter secrecy. It was all mental work and terribly taxing. At the end of a day Sara felt like someone had flattened her brain with a sledgehammer. Sometimes, just talking with her parents required more effort than she could summon. But every night before she went to bed she took out her Earth pouch, held it in the palm of her hand, and pictured the Earth spinning in space. Sometimes she imagined herself standing next to the ocean or high on a mountaintop watching big fluffy clouds drift by. There was hardly ever a breeze on Earth Colony, but whenever Sara held her Earth pouch and pictured herself on Earth, she could feel a playful wind puffing out her clothes and tossing her hair.

*   *   *

Three weeks after Matt's departure from Earth Colony, Sara was convinced that they were ready to reprogram another orb. "This time we'll be able to turn off that dumb alarm," she assured Ryan.

As usual Ryan wanted to follow a cautious step-by-step procedure. "There's more theoretical work to be done here. It may take months," he insisted.

Sara scowled and pulled a sheet of paper from her pocket on which were written a series of equations. Ryan took the paper and scanned it.

"Brilliant, absolutely brilliant! It may work. But we can't be sure." He threw the paper back at Sara.

Sara picked up the paper. "You're a quitter! That's what you are!"

"And you're dangerous!" snapped Ryan.

"But we don't have time to figure it all out. Matt may be out there waiting for our help. The quickest way to proceed is to test as we go along."

"But the orbs probably suspect us already," argued Ryan.

"Nonsense," insisted Sara. "We hardly hung out with Matt at all. There's no reason whatsoever for the orbs to connect us with Cyber or Matt."

"Yes, there is," said Ryan. "Yesterday, my father realized that his transphaser was gone and reported it missing."

Sara hadn't counted on this new piece of information.

"Why didn't you tell me this sooner?" she asked.

"I didn't want to worry you," replied Ryan.

"For your information, I don't want to be protected that way," snapped Sara. "Is there any way we can sneak the transphaser back into your father's medical bag?"

"Sure," replied Ryan, "but we can't reprogram without it."

"Then we have no choice. We have to reprogram as soon as we can!"

Ryan attempted to mount a logical argument against Sara's decision to reprogram, but in the end he relented. "Okay, we'll try one more time, your way. But if it doesn't work, we don't reprogram again until I say so!"

"Fair enough," agreed Sara. "We'll do it in the new forest."

The following day Ryan and Sara told their parents they were going to Luna Park. But after an early breakfast they rode their portabikes out of town. The new forest, adjacent to the old forest, was an undeveloped section of Earth Colony. Usually single orbs with nothing to do were sent there to plant saplings.

"Let's go over the procedure again," said Ryan as

he shoved his collapsed portabike into his backpack. "You have the stopwatch?"

Without saying anything, Sara reached into her pocket, pulled out her father's stopwatch, and held it up for Ryan to see.

"We'll try the kinetic approach for the first three levels and then adjust frequencies, depending on the ratio response," said Ryan.

"Why are you going over this again?" asked Sara. "We both know it by heart."

"Doesn't matter. We've got to be methodical. As soon as we see a lone orb you lie down on the ground and pretend you're hurt. He'll come over to see what's wrong. That will bring him in range and keep him busy while I work the computer. Every second counts. . . ."

Sara was only half listening to Ryan. "Remember when we were little kids and used to play around here?" she said as they entered the forest. "We would play among the trees and make-believe we were on Earth. You'd pretend we were archaeologists looking for fossils, or sometimes we'd be Pilgrims having a hard time making it through that first winter, remember?"

"Sure I do, but why bring up that little kid stuff now? We've got work to do." In spite of himself, Ryan let his mind drift back to when he was much younger. "We were always pretending that we stole a spaceship and escaped from S-15 back to Earth," he said. "We made-believe the forest was an ocean, and we'd swim in among the trees."

"That was our favorite game!" said Sara.

"Yeah, now I remember. We used to say the same things all the time. When the spaceship was blasting off, you'd say, 'I can't wait to see Earth!' and I'd say, 'And I bet she can't wait to see you.' "

"Look!" Sara pointed to an orb at the edge of the new forest not a hundred feet from where they were walking.

The orb was busy levitating saplings out of a bullet and digging holes with its lasers.

"Okay, now don't forget, this time we stick to the procedure." Ryan readied the apparatus and positioned himself behind a tree.

As planned, Sara lay down on the ground.

"Help!" she cried just loud enough for the orb to hear her.

The orb turned off its digging lasers and responded at once.

"How may I serve you?" He approached Sara.

"I think I've sprained my ankle."

Sara pretended to be hurt while Ryan worked the computer, feverishly pushing the buttons that sent out the deprogramming signal.

"I will levitate you to my vehicle and take you to the infirmary," said the orb.

Even as it spoke the orb began to wobble and fall to the ground.

This time there was no pink laser to deal with, and the alarm did not go off.

"We did it!" cried Ryan. "No alarm!"

Suddenly Sara keeled over.

"Sara, what's wrong? I know you're glad, but . . ."

Ryan would have said more but the muscles in his jaw went slack. His legs gave way, and he crumpled to the ground in a heap. His heart was pumping normally, but the rest of his body felt like a bowl of Jell-O.

Stun ray, he thought. *They must have hit us with a stun ray.*

Then he saw them: eight orbs. They came out from behind the trees in pairs, their spherical shells gleaming in the mottled light of the forest.

11) Red Berries

Every morning after breakfast Vaata gave Matt a Dar language lesson. He began by pointing to various objects in the cabin and reciting their names.

"Irepta," he said, pointing to the chair.

"Irepta," repeated Matt.

Whenever Matt added a Dar word to his vocabulary, Vaata broke into a little dance. Pretty soon Matt made a game out of seeing how often he could get Vaata to dance.

After the language lesson, Vaata took Matt to work in the moafoa or garden. The moafoa was a plot about a hundred feet square located behind the cabin. There, in neat rows, Vaata grew all the fruits and vegetables he needed for himself and Matt.

Even though Vaata had gardening implements—a shovel, rake, trowel, and hoe—he usually worked the soil with his hands.

"Turba!" was a word Vaata often used as he plunged his strong fingers into the dirt like a spade. At first Matt thought turba meant "work," but then he realized it was the Dar word for love. And Vaata truly did love his moafoa.

In the past Matt found helping his mother in her garden was a chore on a par with taking out the garbage, or sweeping the floor. It seemed like a messy means to get what you really wanted: vegetables and flowers. But working with Vaata in the moafoa felt like helping someone launch a sailboat or open a treasure chest.

Vaata didn't just talk to his plants, he ministered to them, like a priest visiting a sick parishioner. He swooned over the tall purple stalks with the large pink vegetables, as he pulled off the dead leaves, and he cuddled and cooed every tiny seedling as he watered it, like a mother giving her newborn its first bath.

Most of the time his mood was cheerful, but when a plant was not doing well, if a leaf withered or a fruit developed a disease, Vaata would talk in soft gentle tones. In most cases the plant responded, recovering in a few days. Every time a new shoot or blossom appeared, Vaata pranced and danced, hopping up and down like a monkey on a pogo stick.

Around noon every day Vaata stopped work in the moafoa for a light lunch. Often Vaata and Matt just walked into the jungle picking Dar fruits from the trees. But sometimes Vaata made vegetable soup, stirring the contents in a big black kettle on his simple but efficient stone fireplace.

The rest of the day was spent having fun: swimming in the nearby pond of purple water, lying in the sun or playing board games with sticks and stones—intricate Dar versions of checkers and chess. Sometimes Matt felt as if he were on vacation, visiting a strange but wonderful uncle and having a marvelous time. He even fantasized about staying with Vaata for the rest of his life. *Maybe some day I'll write a book.* Life among the Dars. *Too bad Dars don't read.*

Matt also thought about his parents and getting back to Earth Colony. Not a day passed when he didn't say to himself: *It's only a matter of time before Ryan and Sara come to get me.*

Several days after his arrival, Vaata took Matt to visit another Dar household. Most Dars lived alone like Vaata, but a few lived in pairs or even in small groups. The cabin they were visiting was about twice the size of Vaata's. Only three Dars lived there, but that night there were twelve present. When they stepped inside, Vaata pointed to himself and intoned his own name. Then he went around touching each of the other Dars. "Bobora, Dorima, Tilona, Saakte, Ropte . . ." When he got to Matt everyone blinked his eyelids. At first Matt couldn't figure out what Vaata was trying to tell him. Then he got it. Tonight he would receive a Dar name. Up until now Vaata referred to Matt as "Tafaa." Tafaa was a generic term applied to any newly emerged Dar and meant: "from the forest."

After a light snack that all the Dars fed one another, everyone began to sing and dance. Matt watched while the Dars climbed on one another's shoulders, did somersaults, and shook their bodies like dogs shedding water after a swim.

At a certain point in the middle of a solemn dance, all the guests and dancers stopped and turned to Matt. He was sure that the time had arrived to get his Dar name. But no one said or did anything. After what seemed like a terribly long time, the dance resumed. This went on for an hour or so until the room quieted down and the dancing stopped again.

Now I'll get a Dar name, thought Matt.

Once more he waited but nothing happened. Then the Dars began to take individual turns singing and dancing, one after the other. Matt decided to participate. It felt as if they wanted him to, so why not? When it was his turn he stood up, opened his mouth, and started to sing. He sang the first thing that came to mind which happened to be "Yankee Doodle."

"Yankee Doodle went to town a riding on a pony . . ." he sang loud and clear.

It was his favorite song when he was a little boy. He remembered singing it while playing by the brook near his house. As he sang he marched around in a circle.

When he finished, the room grew deathly quiet. No one moved a muscle. No eyelids blinked. It seemed as if everyone had even stopped breathing. Matt was afraid that he had done something terribly wrong. The embarrassing silence rapidly slipped into a scary stillness.

I made a bad mistake. Matt almost bolted for the door. *They know I'm not a Dar. I'm finished here.* Then without warning, all the Dars began to march in a circle singing "Yankee Doodle."

It was the most bizarre sight Matt had ever seen. It took all his self-restraint not to laugh. From then on Matt had a name. They called him "Yankee."

After the naming ceremony that night, Vaata took a shortcut through the forest on their way home.

Matt was feeling very satisfied with himself and his new name. But when they entered the forest he experienced a strange sense of foreboding. Instead of walking a few paces behind Vaata on the path, Matt stayed very close to Vaata's side.

There had been a shower earlier that evening and the forest smelled cool and moist. The delicate ferns underfoot and the small leaves of the tall dark trees were dripping with violet raindrops.

Vaata, as usual, was in a lighthearted mood. He walked with a hopping dance step, three paces forward and one back, swaying to a silent music that only he could hear in his head.

Noticing that the path left the forest just a few hundred yards up ahead, Matt began to relax. Suddenly Vaata stopped, moaned, and dropped to his knees.

"Da gar mo fa?" ("Are you all right?") asked Matt, using one of the very first sentences that Vaata had taught him.

"Daba. Do ma too fa" ("Yes. But he is not"), replied Vaata.

At first Matt had no idea what Vaata was talking

about. Then he saw the hand sticking out of the bushes. It was a very primitive-looking hand covered with bright blue fur.

Vaata acted quickly. Pushing back the bushes he revealed the body of a Galator ape. The creature was unconscious and bleeding from its side where it had been pierced by a long spike.

"Ma gafora!" ("Gather these!") Vaata pulled the red berries from a nearby fern.

Vaata reached under the ape's shoulders and pulled it onto the path. Then he grabbed hold of the spike and gently pulled.

Matt remembered seeing similar spikes growing on the trunks of certain trees in the jungle.

"Ma gafora!" repeated Vaata. This time his voice sounded a note of urgent alarm.

Matt sprang into action, pulling off berries as fast as he could. By the time he had a handful, Vaata had pulled the spike from the ape and cleaned the wound with spit. Then, one by one, Vaata slowly squeezed the berries over the oozing wound. The berries were full of juice and dripped down onto the hole in the ape's side.

The results were instantaneous and utterly amazing. As soon as the juice of the red berry touched the wound, the blood stopped flowing and it began to heal.

Supporting the ape beneath its head, Vaata opened its mouth and squeezed some of the berries into it. The ape swallowed and a moment later opened its eyes and sat up.

Vaata's eyelids were blinking now, but the ape looked startled.

"What are you doing here?" its expression seemed to say. With a loud shriek it pulled back and disappeared into the forest.

Matt still had some of the berries in his hand and was going to put them in the pocket of his robe. But Vaata reached out and made him drop them.

"Doaabaa" ("Poison"), he said.

12) Great Bird

One afternoon, approximately ten weeks after his arrival, Vaata led Matt down the grassy path behind the cabin into the village of the Dars. Except for all the strange-looking flowers growing on the rooftops, the village reminded Matt of a primitive settlement he had seen a long time ago in an old *National Geographic*.

The street was very crowded with other Dars. Everyone seemed to be moving in the same direction. The closer Matt and Vaata got to the center of town, the more crowded the street became.

"Acasota?" ("What's happening?") asked Matt.

"Velazaura," replied Vaata. Through constant exposure and Vaata's patient tutoring, Matt had already mastered the basics of Dar language, but he had yet to encounter the word Velazaura.

The crowd emptied into a parklike square, surrounded by little moss-covered hills that served as benches. Something that looked like an abstract sculpture dominated the very center of the square. The sculpture was constructed of many long poles, stuck together like a pile of giant pickup sticks. Bright orange bundles dangled from the ends of some of the sticks. The bundles were a foot or two in diameter, tapered at both ends, and maybe four or five feet long.

Looks like something special is going to happen, a festival maybe, thought Matt.

As the square rapidly filled with other Dars, Vaata led Matt toward the central sculpture.

As he drew closer, Matt asked, "Lotanga bonaa renataa?" ("What are the bundles?")

"Lotanga reeno feenoma, arabaho doanee, somanee aldo mornaa." ("Inside each bundle a Dar sleeps and grows wings, waiting for the time to be born again and fly to the mountain.")

Vaata pointed to the mountains in the distance. Though he had to guess at a few of the words, Matt understood more or less what Vaata was telling him.

Just then one of the cocoons began to move. It

slowly undulated back and forth until a thin crack appeared at its lower end. The crack lengthened, and the crowd grew silent. The cocoon began to wiggle violently. Then it split apart and the tip of a bright blue wing emerged. Still moist, it glistened in the sunlight. Slowly the rest of the wing followed. Then another wing broke free and a greenish-yellow beak appeared. It sliced down the entire length of the cocoon which heaved, curled back on itself, and fell to the ground. Now Matt was looking at the most stunning creature he had ever seen: a mature Galator, a Great Bird!

As the Galator's feathers dried, its colors became both brighter and more subtle. Blinking its three opal eyes, it looked out over the silent gathering of Dars, opened its beak, and began to warble and sing. The sweet tender crooning of the Great Bird was clean and pure like spring rain washing away old winter snow.

When at last the Great Bird grew quiet, the crowd murmured its deep approval. A Dar wearing a long robe and carrying a small basket emerged from the crowd and climbed up the sculpture. The Great Bird and the Dar stared into each other's eyes for a moment, blinking at one another. Then the bird reached its beak into the basket and withdrew a fruit about the same size and color as a purple plum.

I've never seen one of those before, thought Matt, who by now had grown to love Dar food. *I wonder how it tastes?*

Jerking its head up and outward, the Great Bird flung the plum into the air. The purple fruit flew up in an arc and came down in Matt's direction. Another Dar, closer to the fruit, reached out to catch it. But Matt crouched down and leaped up, kicking back his heels as if snatching a high line drive out of the air.

"Out!" He heard the call of an imaginary umpire and looked down at the purple fruit in his hand.

"Ooohaaa!" the crowd moaned with one voice.

Gee, I wonder if Dars could like baseball? thought Matt. *Maybe I could get a game going here.*

Vaata bowed. "Nuruga" ("Honored one"), he intoned with great respect.

Then everyone in the crowd stepped back from Matt. Holding hands they formed circles within circles and began to dance and chant.

Matt knew some kind of ritual was in progress and that catching the purple fruit was probably a blessing. But he had no idea where it was all leading to. *Maybe my luck's changing. Maybe I won some kind of Dar door prize or something.*

The dancing went on for some time. Vaata entered the circle and approached Matt.

"Corul!" ("Eat!") Vaata took the plum and lifted it to Matt's mouth.

The plum had a delicate fragrance that reminded Matt of nutmeg. Matt took a bite. It was soft and juicy like a tomato, sweet and flavorful like a grape. He took another bite and swallowed.

At that precise moment the Great Bird spread its enormous wings and rose gracefully into the air, soaring toward the mountains.

The dancers chanted faster and louder.

Tastes pretty good, but I wonder why they're making such a big fuss?

The pace of the dance quickened.

Suddenly Matt felt dizzy and his eyes began to close of their own accord.

Something's not right.

Matt's skin felt ice-cold, but inside, his stomach was bursting into flames.

"I'm on fire!" Matt's knees buckled, and he fell to the ground.

When he opened his eyes, Matt found himself hanging from the large sculpture in the center of the square. His arms were folded against his chest, his legs extended. Vaata, standing next to him on the sculpture, was covering him in fine silken threads that came from small glands in the palm of his right hand. With horror, Matt realized that the fruit he had eaten was a preparation for entering the Galator larval stage, and the fine silken threads were the threads of his cocoon!

13) Truth Serum

When the stun ray wore off, Ryan and Sara found themselves sealed in a windowless gray cube.

"I'm pretty sure we're not at Earth Colony anymore." Sara reached up to a triangular slot in the door of the cell just above her head and pulled herself into a sitting position. Then she attempted to stand, but her legs were still too wobbly. "My whole body feels like an overcooked noodle. Can you stand up yet?"

"I think so," replied Ryan. With his feet planted firmly on the floor, Ryan slid his back up the wall until he was standing. Then he reached down to Sara and pulled her up until they were both leaning against the wall.

For a while they just stood there. Then Sara spoke.

"You're angry with me, aren't you?"

Ryan did not reply.

"You think it was all my fault."

Still silent, Ryan stared straight ahead.

"You hate me."

More silence.

"Well?" said Sara, raising her voice.

"Well, what?" replied Ryan at last.

"Well, why don't you say something!" cried Sara.

Ryan turned toward Sara, his eyes boring into her head like two steel drills.

"What do you want me to say? That it wasn't your fault? That you aren't both the smartest and stupidest person I ever met? That I'd like to strangle you with my bare hands? That I hate you? Well there! I just said it!"

As Ryan's words tumbled out, saliva dripped from the corner of his mouth.

"You're drooling," said Sara.

Ryan wiped his mouth with the back of his hand.

"My mouth muscles aren't right yet," he said.

Sara still felt terrible, but she much preferred Ryan's anger to empty silence.

"Sara, I'm scared."

"I'm not scared. The orbs could have killed us

already if they wanted to." Sara squeezed her Earth pouch. "With any luck, they'll just give us a lecture and send us home."

"But they're afraid of us," said Ryan. "Why else would they have used their stun rays?"

Just then a slot in the door slid open and a tray of food levitated into the cell.

"What's this, room service?" Sara reached out, grabbed two synthetic egg sandwiches from the tray, and handed one to Ryan. "Well, at least they don't intend to starve us to death."

"Eat now, die later," said Ryan. As he brought the sandwich to his mouth, the door in the cell opened and an orb floated in. This orb was about twice the size of any orb they had ever seen before. Instead of silver, its surface was a highly polished yellow gold.

Good! thought Sara. *At least now we'll find out what's going to happen to us.*

"Welcome to Orb Central," said the gleaming yellow sphere in a cheerful voice. "I wouldn't eat that sandwich if I were you."

"Why not?" Sara opened her sandwich and looked inside.

"All the food which we've just given you is laced with a powerful truth serum. It will open up your mind and allow us to record every thought and experience you've ever had on a magnetic disk the size of your fingernail. Unfortunately, it also has some unpleasant side effects."

"Like what?" Ryan returned his sandwich to the tray. "Who are you, anyway?"

"Allow me to answer your second question first," said the friendly orb. "You may call me Orb Two. I am the chief administrator here at Orb Central which, as you know, is the spaceport and central logistics center for all of S-15. As to your first question regarding the side effects of the truth serum. It will reduce your cognitive ability by fifty percent. For example, let's say your IQ was a hundred and sixty before lunch. After lunch it would only be . . ."

"You don't have to explain it to us," said Ryan.

"I might after lunch," said Orb Two.

"I don't imagine you have anything else to eat around here." Sara returned her sandwich to the tray.

"Oh, we do, indeed we do!" replied Orb Two. "But I'm afraid you can't have that food until you've told us what we need to know."

"First, tell us why you brought us here?" demanded Sara. "Why couldn't you have questioned us at Earth Colony? What is this box we're in, anyway?"

"May I remind you, you have not been brought here to ask questions but to answer them," replied Orb Two calmly and politely.

"I'm hungry. What do you want to know?" asked Ryan.

"Ryan!" cried Sara, "You can't . . ."

"Oh, yes, I can," said Ryan. "Nobody's going to fry my brains! Not if I can help it."

"But they're afraid of us, you said so yourself!" argued Sara. "As long as we know something they need to know they won't hurt us."

"You flatter yourselves," interrupted Orb Two. "We've examined your equipment. I must say it's very primitive. But you seem to have stumbled upon a very sophisticated reprogramming formula. We need to know what it is. It's a matter of security. I'm sure you understand. We have been programmed to preserve all life-forms, and serve them to the best of our capacity. But we cannot allow anything or anyone to interfere with our mission."

"We won't tell," cried Sara. "We'll starve to death first. Besides, you're bluffing."

Ryan heaved a long pathetic sigh. "Come on, Sara, face facts. We're beat!"

"He's right," said Orb Two. "Besides, we can administer the serum in other ways. We can put it in the air you breathe."

There's nothing they won't do to achieve their ends, thought Ryan. We must have been crazy to think we could outwit them.

"Okay, you win, we'll tell you." Ryan recited Sara's formula.

"No, it's not true! He's lying!" cried Sara.

"Quite the contrary," responded Orb Two, "My voice analyzers indicate that he's telling the truth. You may eat your lunch now."

"But the truth serum . . ." said Ryan.

"Oh, that was just a tactic. Really, the food is quite safe."

Ryan slammed his fist against his thigh. "We've been had!"

"We wouldn't think of hurting you. A mind is such a terrible thing to waste," said Orb Two.

"What are you going to do to us?" asked Sara.

"Since you ask, I see no harm in telling you," replied Orb Two. "In fact, I see no reason why the despacing process can't start right now."

"Despacing process?" said Ryan.

"Yes," replied Orb Two. "It's both a packaging and preservation technique, one which I think you will find particularly interesting. It's based on the fact that atoms, the basic building blocks of matter, are mostly space. This cell is designed to remove most of that space."

"You mean this cell? The room we're in right now?" asked Sara, her voice quivering with fear.

"That's correct," replied Orb Two. "In a split second you'll be reduced to a fraction of your normal size. It will all happen so fast you won't have time to die. All the while you're despaced, you'll be extremely small inert objects, absolutely harmless to us or to anyone else."

14) True Friends

Vaata pumped his arm over Matt's head like a cowboy throwing a lasso, covering everything but Matt's eyes and mouth with the thin white threads streaming from the glands in the palm of his right hand.

"Mogoora, fa gar mora" ("Be calm, for you are honored"), advised Vaata.

Matt's arms were closely pressed against his side, but he managed to twist his hands around and grab hold of the cocoon. *I'll tear my way out of here.* Matt remembered the time his father had buried him in the sand at the beach. He had been struck with claustrophobia, had panicked and screamed to be dug out.

"Nuga mor" ("Let me go"), Matt pleaded with Vaata. Though he yanked and tore at the cocoon, it would not yield.

"Mogoora, fa gar mora." Vaata withdrew a small, hand-carved wooden vessel from the pocket of his robe. Slowly he removed its tight-fitting cap and ceremoniously offered Matt a pinch of the gray powder that was inside.

"Tassum," he said, extending the powder toward Matt's mouth. "Mo macador fayomora" ("Rejoice! Soon you will be one of the winged").

But Matt turned his head away. "No! I'm not what you think!"

Vaata knew that the purple fruit sometimes induced unusual behavior, but never had he witnessed so pronounced a reaction. Nothing quite like this had ever happened before. As the Dars gathered beneath the sculpture, whispering to one another, an orb crossed the street and joined the crowd.

"Let me go! Let me go!" cried Matt in desperation.

Vaata began to sing a Dar lullaby, hoping to calm Matt down. The purple fruit and the soothing song made Matt feel groggy. His mind began to drift. He thought of sitting around the breakfast table in Ohio. He saw his father reading the Sunday paper.

The image of his mother buttering an English muffin hovered in his mind's eye. As Vaata brought the gray powder near Matt's lips, Matt thought his mother was holding out the muffin for him to sample. Vaata's hand drew near and Matt opened his mouth.

"But I'm not a Dar!" Matt suddenly yanked his head back. "I don't belong here at all! I'm from Earth Colony!"

As soon as the orb heard the words Earth Colony, it levitated to Matt.

"Namalee." The orb instructed Vaata to climb down from the sculpture. Then the orb spoke to Matt. "Hold on, Matt, I'll get you out of here in a moment."

Oh no, this orb knows who I am! What should I do now?

"Ma ma moara Yankee" ("My name is Yankee"), said Matt.

"It's okay, you don't have to pretend anymore. It's me, Cyber," said the orb.

"Cyber! Where have you been all this time?" Matt sounded angry, but his reflection in the shiny robot was grinning back at him.

"It's a long story." Cyber extended a laser, and with surgeonlike skill, cut Matt free of the cocoon. "I'll tell you after we get out of here. I have a new bullet. It's parked on the other side of the square. Can you walk?"

"Sure I can walk." Matt slowly climbed down off the orange sculpture and followed Cyber toward his new vehicle.

"Yankee, nas fa grobora?" ("Yankee, where are you going?") called Vaata as he ran to Matt's side.

"Mas Yankee nogora moatooa. Noas ma gulgg" ("I don't belong here. I have to go"), replied Matt. All the lonely feelings that Matt had pushed down and out of sight for so long suddenly rose up and overwhelmed him. *I keep leaving things and people behind. First, Ohio, then New Jersey and Earth Colony, and now Galator Colony. Home is becoming a meaningless word. I want to take someone with me for a change.*

"Can we take Vaata with us?" Matt asked Cyber hopefully.

"If you are asking is it physically possible, then the answer is yes," replied Cyber, "but I would not advise it."

Matt remembered the last time he failed to heed Cyber's advice. Certain dangers were sure to lie ahead. As much as he dreaded parting with his new friend, Matt could not bring himself to risk Vaata's life.

Twice on the way to the bullet, still under the

numbing affect of the purple fruit, Matt stumbled and fell.

Both times Vaata helped Matt to his feet.

"Ta taatroba nofadoa dioanoa. Na bara. Boara boabtafoa da goraboga" ("Perhaps you are not ready to be a winged one. That's okay. You can stay and live with me anyway"), said Vaata, grasping Matt's hand in his own.

"Yankee ma gulga" ("I must go"), said Matt as he climbed into the bullet. The tears streaming from his eyes splashed onto Vaata's hand.

"Durga volumna rionaa bandu. Mishu volumna finoma. Mishu intona minomar" ("There's a power that's working for you. A mighty power. A planet power. It tells me to give you these"), said Vaata, and taking two of the special purple fruits from his robe, he thrust them into the pocket of Matt's robe.

"Maona donard sidobar" ("True friends never part"), said Vaata, and bringing his hand to his head, touched Matt's tears to his own eyes.

Cyber closed the hatch, and the bullet sped away.

Matt felt weary, like an old man climbing a mountain that went up into the clouds and never stopped. *Must be the purple fruit that's making me feel so terrible.* Matt closed his eyes and fell asleep.

Hours later, when the effect of the purple fruit

had worn off, Matt woke up still feeling terrible, still missing Vaata, still feeling sad.

"Could I really have turned into a great bird?" Matt asked Cyber.

"Only if you took the gray powder," replied Cyber.

"What *was* that stuff, anyway?" asked Matt.

"Ordinary soil from the planet of Galator," said Cyber. "Taken by itself, the purple fruit merely opens up the possibilities of genetic reorientation. Without the soil as a catalyst, no metamorphosis can take place."

Matt was silent for a while, remembering how Vaata had danced and sung the first day they met. Vaata was just starting to teach him basic ceremonial dances and songs. Now that would never happen. Even though Matt knew he was going to miss Vaata terribly and for a long time, he was glad Cyber had shown up when he did.

"What took you so long?" he asked.

"After leaving you, I passed through the force field of Galator Colony and aimed my bullet at the vehicle that was pursuing us," said Cyber. "I had anticipated an evasion tactic on their part. Instead, they opened fire. I abandoned ship just a little too late. The other orb and both bullets were utterly destroyed, and I incurred severe damages. It took a great deal of time to repair myself and infiltrate Galator Colony. I had to laser another orb and assume his identity and function."

"What about the alarm?" asked Matt.

"Damaged in the crash," replied Cyber. "I did not repair it."

"That's great news!" exclaimed Matt thinking to himself. *Now we'll be able to sneak back into Earth Colony.*

"Yes, but I also have bad news. Ryan and Sara were captured while trying to reprogram another orb. I don't know the details, but I do know they've been taken to Orb Central. We're on our way there now."

15) Orb Central

Orb Central was a beehive of robotic activity. Everywhere Matt looked, orbs were moving about. They rode in bullets, zipped by in pneumatic tubes, or slowly bumbled along magnetic walkways like eggs on a conveyer belt.

"Are you sure it's really all right for me to be walking around here in the open?" said Matt as he got out of the bullet.

"Alien clients are often brought to Orb Central for experimental purposes, medical testing, and so on. It will be assumed that you are such a specimen," replied Cyber.

"First we'll go to the Data Center and check personnel files, then we'll know exactly what's happened to Ryan and Sara and where they are."

"But there must be some kind of security system here. Won't the files be locked and guarded?" inquired Matt.

"Only against outsiders. All orbs are permitted full access to any and all data," replied Cyber as he led Matt up a long ramp toward a transit tube. Transit tubes were one of Orb Central's main modes of transportation. They consisted of interconnecting columns of reflected magnetic energy which enabled the orbs to transport heavy cargo at high speeds.

Stepping into the transit tube, Matt and Cyber were swept along in the traffic flow. Matt felt as though he were a white blood cell entering the bloodstream of some enormous robotic body. Orbs and their cargo were floating above, below, and all around him. Most of the cargo was inanimate: high-tech paraphernalia, strange liquids in bizarre-shaped containers, spaghetti balls of glowing wire, pulsing globs of viscous gel, all the endless bits and pieces necessary to keep S-15 functioning.

There were some living things, too. Matt saw a ten-foot-wide, pancake-shaped creature with eyes the size of footballs on long stalks and an alien snake which carried a detachable stomach in a pouch.

"What's that?" Matt pointed to a creature which looked like a tree with legs but no leaves.

"Properly speaking that's not a single organism," replied Cyber, "but a whole family of them. They live together as a symbiotic unit: mother, father, and children. The two parents form the trunk and the children constitute various branches."

"This place is *really* neat," said Matt. "I'd like to know more about it."

"That's Orb Central's Medical Facility on your left," said Cyber as they passed by a huge cylindrical building. "The Medical Facility is where research on alien life forms takes place, and that collection of force fields below you on the right is the environmental sector. That's where the special technologies needed to serve the many colonies of S-15 are developed."

Within each of the tiny domes covering only a few acres, Matt could see every manner of climate and terrain. Some of the them were completely filled with water. Others sizzled with a fierce red heat. There were environments of bizarre tropical vegetation and domes containing barren stretches of pink mosses and black rocks, where globular creatures resembling huge puffs of cotton candy thrived in a glowing neon atmosphere.

"Look down there!" Matt pointed to one of the larger domes below them. "That looks like a brontosaurus!"

"It is," replied Cyber.

"From Earth?"

"Of course."

"You mean orbs gathered specimens from Earth that long ago?"

"No," replied Cyber. "The specimen you see was cloned from single cells which were found in the stomach of an insect preserved in amber from prehistoric times."

Matt loved dinosaurs. Though the brontosaurus was scary to look at, even from a safe distance, he wished he could go down and touch it.

Beyond the environmental sector was Orb Central's Synthetics Factory. This structure looked less like a building and more like a chemistry experiment gone wild. It had no walls or any clearly definable demarcation where the inside stopped and the outside began. It was one vast machine of tubes, vials, bubbling vats, and laser tanks. All the materials the orbs needed to run S-15 were synthesized here from S-15's endless supply of green sand. Huge transmuter ovens converted raw silicone into the basic elements of protons, neutrons, and electrons. From this primordial soup, anything from hydrogen to uranium could be constructed. But that was just the first phase of the process. After that, the elements were recombined to form the complex molecules, organic and inorganic, that went into the creation of everything used to accommodate the inhabitants of S-15.

Leaving the Synthetics Factory, Cyber and Matt passed a number of octagonal buildings stacked on top of one another in honeycomb fashion. "Here's where new orbs are manufactured, repaired, and occasionally reprogrammed," explained Cyber. "The Data Center is coming up on your left. We'll be leaving the transit tube there."

The Data Center was near the spaceport, a large flat area with dozens of enormous Silver Pyramids docked in midair.

Matt recognized the Silver Pyramids at once. The umblemished surface of each spaceship gleamed in the sunlight and mirrored the other ships around it. *One of those ships probably brought me here. Maybe someday one of them will take me back.*

Cyber led Matt off the transit tube and told him to wait near the entrance to the spaceport while he used the Data Center.

"You mean just stand here?" asked Matt.

"Yes, stand perfectly still. Other orbs will assume that your guardian left you in a brain-locked condition. If approached, do not respond."

The Data Center was an enormous revolving disc which hovered about twenty feet off the ground. A steady stream of orbs passed beneath it, radioing their special information requests into the disc and receiving whatever data they asked for in a sudden burst of light.

From where Matt stood, he could see a great line of orbs passing beneath the disc in single file. Cyber was about fiftieth in line, but the flow of information was quick and uninterrupted. As soon as one orb received the data it requested, another one slid into place. Cyber's turn came in just a few minutes. He moved into position beneath the disc and was instantly bathed in a flash of data-rich light.

When Cyber returned to Matt, bright blue sparks of static electricity were bouncing around his shell.

"Don't get too close," warned Cyber. "I may have experienced a slight information overload. In addition to data about Ryan and Sara, I filled my memory banks with any and all information that I thought might be useful. In a few seconds, I will have integrated the new data and returned to normal functioning."

Matt waited while the sparks grew less intense and finally subsided.

"Cyber, are you okay now?"

"Yes," replied Cyber, "and I've found out what happened to Ryan and Sara. They've been despaced."

"Despaced? What are you talking about? What's despaced?"

"Despacing is a process in which the space between individual atoms is drastically reduced," explained Cyber. "Ryan and Sara weigh the same as they always did, but now they can fit into the palm of your hand."

Matt was prepared to hear the worst, but what Cyber said merely confused him. "You mean they're dead?"

"No, when properly respaced, they will resume normal functioning."

"Can we get to them? Can *we* respace them?"

"They're in storage vaults not far from here. Once I retrieve them from the vaults, respacing should not be difficult."

"But how can you get into the vaults?" asked Matt.

"I am equipped with the appropriate codes. There's no reason to expect that I would be denied entry. You, however, should remain here. I'll be back in a few minutes. Just follow the same instructions I gave you before."

Cyber left Matt in an out-of-the-way location, but an occasional orb did pass by. One orb, propelling a large glasslike container of what looked like ordinary mud, stopped directly in front of Matt. While the orb made various inquiries in languages that sounded like gibberish to Matt, a pair of eyes emerged from the mud and pressed themselves against the glass.

Matt did as Cyber instructed and did not move or respond in the slightest.

The orb made clicking and beeping noises for a while and then moved on, pushing the strange tank of mud in front of it.

I can't wait to see Mom and Dad, thought Matt. *Maybe tonight I'll get to sleep in my own bed. Tomorrow I'll play baseball and go to Luna Park. In a week or so, after I've been back for a while, this will all seem like a bad dream.*

It was only a matter of minutes before Cyber finally returned, but to Matt, it seemed like a much longer time.

"Good! I'm glad you're back," said Matt, breathlessly remembering how he felt when Cyber left him stranded at Galator Colony. "But where're Ryan and Sara?"

"Right here," replied Cyber.

Only then did Matt notice the two small objects Cyber was levitating in front of him.

16) White Hole

The "objects" that Cyber was levitating looked like nothing Matt had ever seen before. In fact, they didn't look like objects at all but mere blank spots in his vision. The more Matt tried to focus on them, the blurrier they got.

"I thought you said, I mean, is that . . . ?"

"Yes, it's Ryan and Sara, despaced," said Cyber. "Despaced objects warp light in their vicinity like black holes. But I assure you, this is Ryan and Sara and they are quite all right."

"But I thought you were going to respace them!"

"It's better to wait. The sooner we leave S-15, the better. Follow me." Cyber shot out toward the spaceport and Matt ran after him.

"Leave S-15?" cried Matt.

"Of course," replied Cyber. "What did you think we were going to do?"

"I thought we'd go back to Earth Colony."

"An extremely unwise and unsafe course of action," replied Cyber.

"But I want to see my parents," said Matt. "I want to go home!"

"It's possible for us to attempt to return to Earth Colony," said Cyber, "but judging by what happened to Ryan and Sara, I'd say you'd all end up despaced in a matter of hours."

Matt felt pretty stupid. Now that he thought about it, he realized that what Cyber was saying was perfectly obvious. There was no way to go back to how things used to be. No easy road back home. Matt's fate was now irrevocably intertwined with that of Ryan's and Sara's. *They* had to leave S-15, and therefore so did he. But where would they go? Could they escape back to Earth? Or would they have to keep running from star to star, from galaxy to galaxy?

Two large pyramids were parked at the edge of the spaceport, but Cyber headed straight for a smaller pyramid hovering near the center of the field.

"What about those?" Matt pointed to the larger pyramids.

"Relocation vehicles. Much too slow. We'll take this explorer. It's one of the swiftest ships in the fleet."

The explorer was hovering about fifty feet above the ground. Cyber gave the signal and the rectangular portal in the center of its base slid open.

"Get ready, I'm going to levitate you into the ship," said Cyber.

Matt felt a slight pressure all around his body. Then his feet began to lift off the ground.

"Are you quite comfortable?" asked Cyber.

Matt found the sensation of levitation mildly pleasant.

"Yes, feels kind of like swimming underwater, only without the water. What happens if they discover that Ryan and Sara are gone?" asked Matt. "Will a ship be sent after us?"

"The security system was not designed to handle internal defection," replied Cyber. "It's highly unlikely that Ryan and Sara will be missed. As for the explorer, the records will show that it is on a reconnaissance mission, nothing more."

As he drifted steadily upward, Matt kept looking at Ryan and Sara. Try as he might he could not connect the feelings he had for his friends with those two eerie blurs.

Guided by Cyber, Matt floated through the explorer's open portal, up a vertical shaft, and into the control cabin located at the very apex of the ship.

"Can we despace Ryan and Sara now?" asked Matt as Cyber gave the appropriate signal which instantly generated a magnetic force field beneath Matt's feet.

"Yes, but I'd rather wait until we leave S-15," replied the obedient orb.

Cyber immediately activated the ship's energy well and gave the signal for lift-off.

The control cabin was about fourteen feet square with high ceilings and white walls. Above an instrument panel of blinking colored lights, Matt could see the spectacle of Orb Central through the wraparound view screen.

"Should I lie down and brace myself for blast-off?" asked Matt nervously.

"That won't be necessary," said Cyber. "The explorer is equipped with counter G force. You won't feel the slightest sensation of motion."

The explorer began to rise slowly at first, and then rapidly increased its rate of ascent.

Matt watched through the view screen while Orb Central grew smaller and other domes shifted into his field of vision. *There's Galator Colony.* Matt recognized the mountains where the Great Birds lived. The explorer rose still higher until Matt could see Earth Colony. From a distance of ten miles, where the curvature of S-15 was plainly visible, Earth Colony seemed like a very small place indeed. *From up here it looks like a goldfish bowl or a cage in a pet shop.* Matt suddenly found it hard to understand why just a little while ago he felt such an urgent need to return to Earth Colony.

"How long will it take to respace Ryan and Sara?"

"Less than a second. Stand back. I'll attend to it now."

Cyber levitated the two blurs in front of him to about eight inches above the floor of the spacecraft.

Matt stood aside, pressing his back against the control panel.

"Commencing respacement, now!"

Suddenly the two blurs exploded with a loud *swoosh* and Ryan and Sara appeared as if out of nowhere.

"What!" Ryan fell backward, sprawling across the floor, while Sara lurched forward into Matt's arms.

"Matt! Is that. . . ? Are we. . . ?" Ryan and Sara were completely disoriented. As far as they were concerned, Orb 2 had just left their cell and they were about to be despaced.

"It's okay." Matt hugged Sara. "Cyber respaced you. We're on a ship leaving S-15."

"So the reports of your death were greatly exaggerated." Ryan grinned foolishly as he got to his feet.

"And Cyber's fine too." Matt proceeded to fill in Ryan and Sara on what had happened to him since he left Earth Colony.

"Quite a story," said Sara when he finished. "You're lucky to be alive."

"Jumping into that bullet was the stupidest thing I ever saw anyone do," said Ryan. "I'd never do anything that dumb."

"You forget, if it wasn't for Matt we'd still be despaced," said Sara.

Ryan heaved a great sigh and changed the subject. "Where's this spaceship headed for?" he asked Cyber.

"As of yet I haven't set a course," replied Cyber.

"Why not head for Earth?" suggested Sara.

"Extremely inadvisable," answered Cyber. "Eventually Orb Two would track us down and all three of you would be despaced."

"What about escaping to another galaxy?" asked Matt.

They were a trio now. That, after all, is what Matt had wanted in the first place. Whether Ryan and Sara accepted him or not, he was a member of their team and had a right to speak his mind.

"Risky and impractical," said Cyber.

"Okay, so what do you recommend?" said Ryan.

"I recommend we set our course for Terezor," replied Cyber.

"Terezor! What good will that do?" cried Ryan. "Aren't there more orbs on Terezor?"

"Yes, but Orb One also resides there," replied Cyber. "Orb One controls *all* the other orbs in the galaxy. With Sara's formula and my help, I believe it's possible to reprogram Orb One. Given the circumstances, this is the only way to ensure your safety."

"What about the Terezors?" said Sara.

"The Terezors have been extinct for decades," replied Cyber.

"You're joking!" said Sara.

"I only joke when I am . . ."

"I know," said Matt, "when you're requested."

"If that doesn't qualify as a cosmic joke then I don't know what does." Ryan laughed out loud. "The Terezors extinct! Ha! And they wanted to save the rest of the galaxy. Maybe they should have started with saving themselves!"

"What happened to them?" asked Sara. "Did they have a terrible war? Was it ozone depletion? An epidemic disease? The greenhouse effect? A supernova, perhaps?"

"They were engulfed by a White Hole," replied Cyber.

"A White Hole!" exclaimed Sara. "What's that?"

"Your scientists, as yet, have not encountered White Holes," replied Cyber. "Unfortunately the Terezors did not know what they were either, until it was too late."

"So what are they?" asked Matt.

"White Holes are whole regions of space where black holes from parallel worlds impinge on this reality," said Cyber. "As might be expected, they obey none of the usual laws of physics. Indeed their individual natures depend entirely on the characteristics of the worlds they come from. The particular White Hole that engulfed Terezor affected only the Terezors."

"I still don't get it," said Matt. "What happened to the Terezors?"

"Quite simply," continued Cyber, "as the entire planetary system of Terezor traveled through the White Hole, the Terezors disappeared into another universe. One moment they were a thriving, well-adjusted race, and the next, they were gone."

"All of them?" asked Sara.

"Every last one," replied Cyber. "Since that time we've had no contact whatsoever from the Terezors."

"So the orbs have been carrying on by themselves, like a TV that stays on when you leave the room?" asked Matt.

"That's correct," replied Cyber. "That's why I believe it's entirely feasible for you to reprogram Orb One and take charge."

For a moment all three were silent.

Finally it was Sara who spoke. "Well, Cyber"—Sara reached for her Earth pouch and gently squeezed it—"I guess we have no choice. Set our course for Terezor!"

17) Star Drive

"How long will it take the explorer to get to Terezor?" asked Matt.

"Approximately twenty minutes," replied Cyber.

"Then it must be fairly close," said Matt.

"It's two hundred and forty-three light-years away," replied Cyber.

"Then the explorer must go millions of times faster than the speed of light," said Ryan.

"No, it is impossible to exceed the speed of light," replied Cyber.

Matt was now totally confused. "Isn't a light-year the distance light travels in a year?"

"That's correct," replied Cyber.

"Then I don't get it. How can we get to Terezor

in a matter of minutes if its two hundred and forty-three light-years away, and we can't go faster than the speed of light?"

"Well put," said Ryan. "I must say I'm rather surprised that someone like you knows what a light-year is."

Someone like me? Matt was indignant. "For your information . . ."

"Hey, cut it out you two!" protested Sara. "I want to hear what Cyber has to say."

"Perhaps it's best if I explain in simple language," continued Cyber. "Let's say you want to go from point *A* to point *B*. The faster you go, the quicker you'll get there. But at a certain point you can't go any faster. That's the speed of light. If you want to get there quicker, you have to move point *A* closer to point *B*. That's how the explorer's star drive works, by condensing or shrinking the space between us and our destination. As a matter of fact, we're moving into space condensation mode now. If you look out the viewer, you'll see the visual effects of the process."

"Looks the same to me," said Matt. "Bright little stars against a black backdrop."

"Keep looking," said Cyber. "Notice the deep purple tones forming like halos around the stars."

"Yes, I see them!" cried Sara. "It's lovely!"

"In a matter of seconds we'll be entering condensed space," announced Cyber.

All of a sudden, the scene outside the viewer changed dramatically. Space ceased to be a black void but swept past in huge sheets of bright color. Explosions of orange, pink, green, and fuchsia light bathed the interior of the explorer's control cabin and rippled across their faces.

"I've never seen anything so pretty," said Sara. "It's like Mardi Gras in New Orleans."

"How would you know? You've never been to the Mardi Gras," said Ryan.

"No, but I've seen it on holovision," responded Sara.

Every few seconds the control cabin was again filled with the intense pulse of rainbow-colored light.

"That's what a star looks like in condensed space," explained Cyber.

For awhile the trio just stared out the viewer, totally absorbed in the spellbinding sight of condensed space.

"What about Terezor?" Ryan, unable to put practical matters aside for very long, was the first to look away from the viewer. "Shouldn't we have a plan? I mean, what are we going to do when we get there?"

"I've already formulated a strategy," responded

Cyber. "The explorer is a reconnaissance vehicle. Its function is to seek out and explore new planets. I will claim that I've just discovered a new planet in need of protection. According to standard rules of procedure, I am required to report such a discovery directly to Orb One. Of course, as soon as I gain access to Orb One, instead of making a report, I will use Sara's formula to reprogram Orb One in the same way I was reprogrammed."

"Sounds good to me," said Matt.

"What's our part in all this?" asked Ryan suspiciously.

"You three will serve as specimens of the new alien race that I've just discovered," replied Cyber. "It's standard procedure to bring along such specimens."

"But we're obviously human," said Ryan. "Won't Orb One be suspicious?"

"Many alien species are basically humanoid in appearance," replied Cyber. "Without detailed analysis there's no way for Orb One to know your real identity."

"Seems like a pretty good plan to me," said Sara.

"I agree," said Matt.

"Won't there be a security check when we land?" inquired Ryan.

"That's standard procedure," replied Cyber.

"Could there be any problems with that?" asked Ryan.

"I don't anticipate any," replied Cyber.

Ryan stared at Cyber but didn't say anything.

"Any more questions?" asked Cyber.

"No, but I'm worried," declared Ryan.

"That's nothing new. You worry all the time," said Sara. "You're going to have gray hairs before you're fourteen!"

"If I live that long," said Ryan.

As the explorer neared its destination, space took on its conventional appearance. The bright colors of condensed space faded and the austere black void once again asserted itself. The stars, like diamonds in a jeweler's velvet case, slipped back into normal perspective. Shining a hundred times more brightly than any other stars, one huge green ball of light drifted into view.

"We are now in the planetary system of Terezor," announced Cyber.

"That green star? That's Terezor's sun?" asked Matt.

"Yes, I'm putting a filter on the view screen so you can look at it without harming your retinas," said Cyber. "Presently it's eclipsing one of its seven planets, but as we draw closer you'll be able to see the other six."

"Which one of those planets is Terezor?" asked Matt.

"Terezor is not a single planet but a planetary complex," responded Cyber. "The original Terezor was the fourth planet from its sun. When technology permitted, the orbits of the other six planets were altered to conform with the fourth planet. Then atmospheres were added and they became habitable."

"You mean the Terezors moved the other planets of their solar system into their own orbit so they could live on them?" asked Matt.

"That's correct," replied Cyber. "This assured the Terezors optimum conditions for expansion within the confines of their own solar system."

"Then there are seven Terezors?" said Sara.

"Also correct," replied Cyber.

"But there are no Terezors on any of them. Is that right?" asked Matt.

"As I said before, they all disappeared when the planetary complex entered a White Hole," replied Cyber.

"On which planet is Orb One's headquarters?" asked Ryan.

"Orb One is based on Terezor Four," replied Cyber.

Except for size, all the planets of Terezor had a similar appearance. Their irregular continents had been re-formed into huge strips of land that circled the entire globe. Alternating with wide channels of sea, these artificially constructed land masses ran parallel to each planet's equator and were mainly located in the northern and southern temperate zones. Most of the strips appeared to be solid green in color. These were Terezor's forests. Population zones varied in appearance but were mostly gray.

"Look, the clouds are square!" said Matt as they drew closer to Terezor Four.

"That makes them easier to measure and manage," said Cyber. "We've been contacted by Spaceport Control and cleared to land at sector K. Also I am pleased to report that my request for an immediate meeting with Orb One has been granted."

"I don't like this," said Ryan. "Everything's going according to plan."

"What's wrong with that?" asked Matt.

Ryan did not reply.

Descending through a square cloud bank, the explorer docked at Terezor Four's high-security spaceport.

Though the Terezors were extinct, the orbs had kept the planet in good working order. The city near the spaceport, for example, was just as the

Terezors had left it. The buildings, force field
spheres of iridescent pink, were all well maintained
even though there was no one living in them. The
transit tubes ran perfectly on time, but were empty.
The parks were well trimmed, but unattended, the
fountains were beautiful, but unadmired.

As the explorer set down, a gray disc approached.
The disc reminded Matt of a giant checker. It was
about five yards wide, a foot thick, and hovered just
a few feet above the ground.

"What's that?" asked Matt.

"The Terezor equivalent of a taxicab. It was sent
to take us directly to Orb One," reported Cyber.
"Prepare for levitation. I'm going to withdraw the
floor now."

"How do you like levitating?" Matt asked Sara as
Cyber lowered them out of the explorer and onto
the transport disc.

"It tickles a little," said Sara, "but I like it."

When they were all aboard the disc, Cyber took
over the controls.

"Prepare to disembark."

A split second later they were traveling at super-
sonic speeds toward Terezor's government complex
and Orb One's Headquarters.

18) Royal Robot

Terezor's Government Complex was an intricate collection of huge geometric buildings offset by grand and elaborate expanses of colorful vegetation, cascading waterfalls, and shooting fountains.

"The disc will take us directly to Orb One's Headquarters," said Cyber. "That's the large sphere directly ahead of us."

Orb Headquarters was an enormous structure, approximately half a mile in diameter. In many ways it resembled an enormous orb. Like an orb, to even the keenest observer, its highly polished silver surface revealed nothing of its internal structure. The closer one looked, the more one saw of oneself.

"What's in there besides Orb One?" asked Matt.

"Orb One's Headquarters is divided into chambers like a beehive," replied Cyber. "Orb One resides in the central chamber like the queen bee. In the other chambers thousands of other orbs perform various duties to assist Orb One. They're like the worker bees. And of course there's the data, the honey of the hive. Data, data, and more data; all the data Orb One needs to control the galaxy."

"It must be the largest data bank in the whole world," said Sara.

"Definitely the largest in the galaxy," said Cyber.

Matt watched while the reflected image of the disc moved across the surface of Orb Headquarters like a small bug flying in front of the Moon.

"I hope you know what you're doing, Cyber," said Ryan as they flew through an arched doorway. Upon entering the spherical building, they gently came to rest on a metallic platform just outside Orb One's chamber.

"I have dedicated all my circuits to this task," replied Cyber. "I can do no more."

Matt was experiencing a peculiar kind of fear. It was like the panic he experienced in the cocoon, the horror of the red fish, and the chill he felt when he first met Vaata. But it was also different from all those fears. It was the fear of taking on too much power. *What if we succeed? What if we take over Orb One and the whole galaxy? What then?*

Cyber turned off the force field and one by one they stepped off the disc.

There were no windows in the chamber, but its metallic walls glowed with an internal source of light. It was a harsh blue light not intended for human eyes. To see at all, they had to squint.

Two orbs came forward, and Cyber conferred electronically with them.

"Who are they?" asked Sara.

"Orb One's secretaries," said Cyber. "They say Orb One has had a change of plans. He's too busy to see us today. They want us to come back tomorrow."

"Good," said Ryan, "that will give us time to think this through."

"Yes, tell them we'll come back tomorrow," said Sara.

Matt was surprised to hear Sara talking like that. Usually she was the one who wanted to forge ahead at all cost.

"Sorry, but I've already told them it's an emergency," said Cyber.

Without warning the wall behind them parted, revealing a huge domed hall. In the center of the hall, midway between the floor and the ceiling, Orb

One hovered in a beam of white light. Orb One was neither silver nor gold, but an enormous globe of glowing lights, throbbing discharges, and electromagnetic pulses. Some twelve feet in diameter, Orb One loomed above them like a precious multicolored gem in a setting of radiant light.

Orb One looks royal, thought Matt. *Like a king! Like a god!*

Now that he had seen Orb One, Ryan was convinced Cyber's plan was not going to work.

"It's like sicking a goldfish on a shark," he whispered to Sara.

"I'm not worried; Cyber knows what he's doing," said Sara, but to herself she thought, *My formula was made for reprogramming an ordinary orb, and something tells me Orb One has more than seven levels.*

Cyber began the reprogramming process at once. But no sooner did he beam the first part of Sara's formula at Orb One, than Orb One intercepted his signals and beamed a powerful laser back at him.

The laser bored a hole right through Cyber's shell. *Bam!* It was all over in an instant. Cyber fell to the floor in a puff of blue smoke.

"I believe your holiday has come to an end," said Orb One in ever so pleasant a voice.

"I told you we weren't ready for this," cried Ryan. "Now everything's out of control again!"

"No, everything is under control again," replied Orb One.

Two guard orbs entered the chamber and levitated Cyber off the floor.

"What's happened to our orb?" demanded Matt.

"It's been decommissioned," replied Orb One. "Now, if you'll follow these guards to the despacing cell, I will return to my duties."

When the two guard orbs grabbed hold of Sara with their magnetic grippers, she pulled back.

"Get your force fields off me!" she cried.

"Very well, then," said one of the guard orbs. "Right this way."

The despacing rooms were located in a huge silo-shaped building below Orb One's Headquarters. To get there they had to pass through a transit tube and down a long narrow walk. On either side of the walk at about waist level all manner of Terezor flowers and shrubbery were growing in raised planters. The unusual Terezor greenery caught Matt's eye. He reached out and picked a Terezor flower for Sara. It was a white flower with orange bumps on its petals. He had meant to break the flower off at the stem but the entire plant came out of the ground, roots and all.

"Thanks." Sara accepted the flower with a sad sort of smile.

Once inside the building, the guard orbs led them down a long narrow corridor.

"Feels like a prison," said Matt.

"It is a prison," said Ryan bitterly, "our prison!"

"Stop here," said one of the orbs. A door beside them opened. Behind the door was a storage room with all kinds of electronic spare parts piled on the floor. The guard orb that was carrying Cyber tossed him into the room like a tin can on a scrap heap.

"Good-bye, Cyber," said Matt, "thanks for trying." Matt felt like crying. *It's silly to grieve. Cyber was only a machine*, Matt told himself, but the feeling was there just the same.

The door closed, and they moved on.

At the end of the corridor, another door opened.

"Enter," said the guard orb.

"Look familiar?" said Ryan, his voice full of sarcasm.

"Very familiar," sighed Sara as the door slid shut behind them. "Exactly the same as the one at Orb Central."

"So this is the despacing chamber?" Matt sat down on the floor. "Does it hurt to be despaced?"

"I didn't feel a thing," said Ryan.

"Me either," said Sara.

Soon a deathly silence prevailed. There seemed to be nothing to say, nothing to do, but wait.

Some time later, one of the guard orbs entered with a tray of food.

"Uh-oh," said Ryan, "looks like another trick."

"No tricks. Orb One has decided to study you for a while prior to despacing. We hope you find this food to your liking," said the guard orb as it left the cell.

Ryan picked up one of the food cubes and tasted it. "Not bad, if you like dog biscuits."

"We should have eaten the egg sandwiches when we had a chance," said Sara.

Strangely enough, now that they had failed, everyone felt more relaxed. They had reached the bottom. There was nowhere left to fall.

Matt picked up one of the food cubes. He was hungry but couldn't bring himself to eat it. "You wouldn't believe the delicious fruits they grow on Galator. They were . . . scrumptious."

"Please don't talk about them," said Ryan. "I just ate one of those cubes, so I'm not in the mood to hear about anything that tastes good."

Matt remembered the two purple fruits in his robe.

"There's a power that's working for you. A mighty power. A planet power." Vaata's words echoed in Matt's mind as he took the fruits from his robe.

"I have two fruits from Galator Colony; they're still firm and fresh but we can't eat them." Matt explained in great detail what happened that day when the Great Bird came out of its cocoon. As he spoke Sara listened intently.

"Yes! Planet power," exclaimed Sara when Matt finished. "That's it! That's how I feel about my Earth pouch. It puts me in touch with the power of the Earth!"

Closing her eyes, Sara gently squeezed her Earth pouch.

"You and that silly pouch of yours," grumbled Ryan. "If it had any power, then how come we're in such trouble?"

Sara didn't respond but sat perfectly still. In her mind she pictured the Earth, swirling white clouds above a blue-green disc. *Can you help us?* she whispered to the Earth and an answer came. Opening her eyes she held up the flower Matt had given her and smiled.

"Look, there's soil on the roots. That's all we need!"

"All we need?" asked Matt.

"That purple fruit, this flower, and some soil from my Earth pouch." Sara was now grinning. "That's all we need to get out of here!"

19) Twelve Arms

"Sara, what are you talking about?" Ryan looked at Sara as if she'd gone mad.

"Only something a *scientist* like you should have figured out already," answered Sara. "If the purple fruit and Galator soil, acting as a catalyst, can change a Dar into a Great Bird, then there's no reason why one of us can't use the purple fruit with Terezor soil and change into a Terezor!"

"That's the stupidest thing I've ever heard," said Ryan with a yawn. "I'm getting sleepy."

"You still haven't answered my question," pressed Sara.

"It just won't work," said Ryan as he stretched

out on the floor, using his arm as a pillow. "We're not Dars. Our metabolism is different."

"But you heard what happened when Matt ate the purple fruit. His body reacted *as if* he were a Dar. And Cyber said if he swallowed the Galator soil, he would have metamorphosed into a mature Galator!"

"Yes, but we don't know that Terezor soil would have the same catalytic effect," said Ryan.

"No, of course we don't. But we do know if we don't try, we're sure to get despaced!" said Sara.

"But even if it does work and one of us changes into a Terezor, what good will it do?" asked Ryan.

"Don't you see?" Sara wrung her hands in exasperation. "The Terezors created Orb One. Once one of us *is* a Terezor we can figure out how to control it!"

"Sara's starting to make sense, but if anyone's going to attempt this it ought to be me," said Matt. "I've been eating nothing but Galator food for months. My body's already adjusted."

"It would be just like you to make a stupid move like that," said Ryan. "Don't blame me if you get stuck in the body of a Terezor."

"There are two purple fruits," said Sara. "With the other purple fruit and the soil from my Earth pouch, the whole process can be reversed."

"Very clever, but what if *that* doesn't work?" said Ryan.

"It's got to work!" insisted Sara.

"It's worth a try." Matt popped the purple fruit into his mouth, chewed slowly, and swallowed.

"Mmm, tastes delicious. At least now I won't have to eat any of those dog biscuits."

"How long before it takes effect?" asked Sara.

"Seconds," said Matt, sensing his heart thumping faster and his skin begining to chill. "I'll probably pass out shortly. When I revive, give me the Terezor soil. I may act a little weird at times, but don't mind that." Matt lay down on the floor, closed his eyes, and braced himself, knowing that the flames would soon ignite in his stomach.

Sara took the flower and knocked the dirt from its roots into her hand.

A few minutes later, Matt opened his eyes.

"I'm falling into a cloud. My legs are like black-berries and I can sing upside down and think backward."

"That's wonderful, you're doing just fine," said Sara. She held the Terezor soil up to Matt's face. "Here, swallow this."

Matt stared blankly into space, so Sara opened his jaw and poured the dirt in.

"Tastes salty."

"Just swallow," urged Sara.

Matt swallowed. "Tastes salty, like sailboats and popcorn."

"You're both crazy!" murmured Ryan as he rolled over and drifted off to sleep.

Matt's mind was in a hazy state of reverie until the catalytic action of the Terezor soil started to take hold. In a few minutes, he sank into a deep coma. While he slept unawares, his entire metabolism began to undergo dramatic changes. His endocrine system started pumping out enzymes that sent chemical messages to the blood-producing cells in the marrow of his bones. The synapses in his brain cells fused together. Some organs began to atrophy. Others began to grow. For a long time, however, there were no external changes.

"Wake up, Ryan." Sara grabbed Ryan by the shoulders and shook him.

Ryan opened his eyes slowly.

"What do you want?"

"Matt's asleep," said Sara.

"You woke me up to tell me that!" Ryan rolled over and went back to sleep.

Sara stared at Matt for over an hour, waiting for any sign that he was beginning to metamorphose. When none came, she too lay down and closed her eyes.

"You know, for a moment there, I thought I was making sense," thought Sara to herself as she dropped off to sleep.

While Ryan and Sara slept, Matt continued to

undergo an incredible biological metamorphosis.

A thick scaly skin grew over his entire body. The bones in his legs dissolved into basic calcium and flowed through his new bloodstream to other parts of his body. His head absorbed his hair and grew down into his shoulders. His eyes grew across the bridge of his nose and merged together into a band that eventually circled his entire skull. His mouth disappeared, relocating itself near his navel. In a few hours his body took on an overall globular shape, his legs atrophied into stumps and then disappeared entirely, new arms began to grow, and he started breathing through his skin.

When Matt finally awoke he opened his one enormous eye and thought he was dreaming. Not only could he see what lay in front of him, but he could see what lay behind him. He could see everything around him, all 360 degrees of it.

He felt like laughing and heard a strange sound coming from his stomach. *I guess that's where my mouth is now,* he thought to himself.

Six different kinds of appendages were at the end of his twelve arms. One by one he held them up and examined them. Two were like human hands. Two others had hooklike attachments. Two had suction cups. Another two were blunt, like hammers, with tiny delicate feelers.

So this is a Terezor; not exactly cute.

Pulling his arms around his torso, he found that he could compose himself into a perfectly round ball.

No wonder their robots are spheres. The Terezors made them in the image of themselves.

No legs. I wonder how Terezors move. Do they roll? No, that doesn't feel right. Perhaps they levitate!

Matt willed himself into the air and floated up off the floor. *It's easy. Same as moving an arm or a leg in my normal body. Now for speech.*

Matt sensed his new Terezor mind was like a house with many rooms. Moving from room to room he tried to find that part of his new brain devoted to speech. Of course, he knew nothing of the Terezor language. But the Terezor mechanisms for forming intelligible sounds were not unlike those of the human voice box. Looking down, he saw Ryan and Sara still asleep on the floor beneath him.

"Waaaarrkkk urrpppp. Waaakkk urp. Waaake uuuup. Wake up!"

Ryan was the first to open his eyes.

"Aaaaah!" he screamed as he sat bolt upright, thinking that a terrible monster had somehow slipped out of his dreams.

20) Orange Beam

Still groggy from sleep, Sara screamed, "Haaaa! Get it away from me!"

Then she saw Matt's robe lying on the floor beneath the Terezor.

"It's okay, I mean I think it's okay, I mean, I think it's Matt!" Sara got to her feet cautiously.

"The purple fruit. *It worked?*" exclaimed Ryan.

"I think so." Sara took a baby step closer to the Terezor. "Matt, is that you?" Her voice trembled with fear. Though Sara wanted to reach out, she dared not touch the creature Matt had become.

"Yeeaa . . . Yeaa . . . Yesssss," said Matt.

"Matt, are you okay?" asked Sara.

"Yesss," said Matt, pleased that his ability to

operate his organs of speech was already improving.

"What an incredible creature!" Ryan, having recovered from his initial shock, stepped closer. "He's got twelve arms with six different functions, and just look at that eye! I'll bet he can see a full three hundred and sixty degrees in every direction. I wish I had a notebook or at least a camera to take pictures."

"Pictures aren't going to do us any good if we don't get out of here," said Sara. "We have to have a plan."

"A plan!" exclaimed Ryan. "A plan for what? Matt's altered his body, that's all. He doesn't know anything more than he did before. He probably can't even get us out of this cell."

"What about it?" Sara turned to Matt. "Can you get us out of here?"

Matt had a new body and he also had a new brain, a Terezor brain, perhaps the most developed organic thinking machine in the entire galaxy. While Matt was thinking about how to use his new brain, it had already solved the problem of getting out of the despacing chamber and was working on the problem of communicating that solution to Matt. Suddenly, as if it were displaying a piece of data on a computer monitor, Matt's brain brought the triangular indentation in the door of the cell into sharp focus. *Why am I seeing that so clearly?* wondered Matt. Then for no apparent reason, Matt felt a tingling sensation in one of his appendages. As he raised that arm to see what was wrong with it, he realized that the triangular-shaped appendage exactly matched the triangular-indentation in the door.

He slowly levitated toward the door and awkwardly placed the triangular-shaped hand in the similarly shaped slot.

"Look," exclaimed Sara, "Matt has a hand that fits the door like a key!"

The door was probably designed that way so Terezors could never get trapped in their own despacing chambers! thought Matt.

Matt's control of his arm was shaky at best. He awkwardly turned it one way and then the other with no results.

"Try pushing," suggested Sara.

Matt pushed, and the door slid open.

"We're out!" cried Sara.

"I don't believe it!" mumbled Ryan.

Matt felt a distinct pleasure knowing that now with his new Terezor brain he was actually smarter than Ryan. But he wondered: *Can I outsmart Orb One?*

Thinking that there was no way his prisoners could escape, Orb One had not bothered to place a guard at the other side of the door.

"Now what?" said Ryan, following Matt and Sara into the corridor.

Matt felt his new Terezor mind gently probing his human mind, sifting through his thoughts like a miner panning for gold. It was an awkward sensation but not unpleasant. Suddenly the single word *"Cyber!"* popped out of his abdominal mouth.

"Cyber? Cyber's no good to us now," cried Ryan. "He's been decommissioned."

But Matt was already floating down the corridor toward Cyber's door.

This time he placed his hand in the triangular slot and opened the door without Sara's help. Cyber was lying exactly where the guard orbs had left him on a scrap heap of electronic innards. Matt floated into the cubicle and picked up Cyber with his two human-looking hands.

"I get it," said Sara, "Matt wants to get Cyber working again so Cyber can give him the proper Terezor commands he needs in order to deal with Orb One."

"Give Cyber to me," said Ryan, at last realizing that if they were going to get out of this alive, they had to work as a true team.

Ryan peered into the hole Orb One had blasted into Cyber's shell.

"Look, that terminal is melted. It's probably the hookup to Cyber's main power supply. If we just had a laser torch, I could reconnect it."

One of Matt's arms ended in a ball of mirrored surfaces. He held it up to his eye and examined it. At the same time, he ran through the many rooms of his new Terezor mind until he found the room that dealt with the use of this particular appendage.

"Lassser!" he said, and a thin pink beam shot forth from the mirrored ball, drilling a hole in the wall.

"Good golly, the Terezors were born with lasers!" cried Sara.

"Yes, but can Matt control it?" said Ryan, grabbing Matt's laser arm. "It's too powerful, can you turn it down?"

It took some practice, but in a little while Matt learned to make subtle adjustments in the power output of his laser.

"Okay, we're ready now."

Ryan held on to Matt's wrist and guided the laser inside Cyber's shell. "Start with a low beam, and then turn it up step by step. I'll call out the numbers. Ready? one, two, three . . ."

Suddenly Cyber's power supply was reconnected, and he sprang back into operation.

"Ryan, Sara, where are we? What's happened? Where's Matt?"

"Matt's right in front of you," said Sara.

"I'm sorry, but you are grossly mistaken." Cyber shot an orange beam of light into Matt's eye.

"Cyber, stop." Ryan thought for a split second that Cyber was attacking Matt.

"No need for alarm," replied Cyber. "I only wanted to make sure that the creature before me was actually a Terezor. The orange laser is an identification beam used for that specific purpose."

"But it's not a Terezor," said Sara, "it's Matt."

"That assertion does not compute," said Cyber. "The creature before me *is* a Terezor."

"No, it's not, it's Matt," countered Sara.

"Stop arguing," insisted Ryan. "The important thing is to figure out what to do next."

"Yes," said Matt.

"This Terezor speaks English," said Cyber. "I find that very unusual."

"It's not a Terezor! It's Matt," insisted Ryan, nearly screaming.

"Not so loud!" Sara shushed him.

"BRAXIS VAX NIZIM," said Cyber to Matt.

"What did you say?" said Sara.

"I asked him if he was a Terezor," said Cyber, "but so far he hasn't responded."

"And he won't either," said Ryan. "It's Matt. He doesn't know how to speak Terezor."

"Extraordinary!" said Cyber. "Is it really you, Matt?"

"Yes," said Matt.

"He ate the purple fruit of Galator and some Terezor soil."

"Extraordinary," said Cyber.

"Is that all you can do? Say extraordinary?" cried Sara.

"What would you like me to do?" asked Cyber.

"You know how to speak Terezor, don't you?" said Sara.

"Yes," replied Cyber.

"Teach him enough Terezor to take control of Orb One," said Ryan.

"An excellent idea," said Cyber. "Where would you like to begin?"

"Teach him how to turn Orb One off," said Sara.

"NAX!" said Cyber.

"NAX," repeated Matt.

"What's it mean?" asked Ryan.

"NAX means stop," said Cyber. "Any orb hearing that command from a Terezor will automatically shut down all systems."

"Even Orb One?" said Sara.

"Yes, I believe so, but first he'll test with his identification beam to make sure Matt is really a Terezor."

"That sounds risky to me," said Ryan. "We fooled Cyber but Orb One is bound to know the difference."

"I'mmmm g-g-going," said Matt.

"Wait, we'll come with you," cried Sara.

"No, you should wait here," instructed Cyber. "If seen, you'll be treated as an escaped prisoner and shot on sight."

"Wait." Sara took the Earth pouch from her neck and ran up to Matt. Standing on tiptoes, she hung it around the spot where his neck should have been.

"This will bring you good luck," she said.

Still unsure of his powers of levitation, Matt bounced off the walls as he drifted down the corridor.

As he reached the exit of the cylinder-shaped building he encountered an orb guarding the door.

"NAX!"

The orb shot an orange beam of light into his eye and fell to the ground.

This is going to be easy. Matt continued toward the huge sphere that was Orb One's Headquarters.

He had a distance of about the length of a football field to traverse. As he floated along, he realized he could move much faster if he thought of himself as running.

I'll bet I could go a hundred miles an hour in this body, no trouble. Though he had mastered speed, he was not so practiced at stopping. Unable to slow himself down in time, he slammed with a thud into the portal door of Orb One's Headquarters.

He slid down the surface of the door and fell to the ground. Before he could rise, the orbs on the other side gave the signal for the door to open.

"NAX!" said Matt. Both orbs shot their orange identification beams at his forehead, turned off, and fell to the ground.

Matt floated down the long corridor toward Orb One's chambers.

"NAX!" He disarmed Orb One's guards.

This is fun, thought Matt as the great wall of the chamber began to open.

Orb One's sensors told it that a threatening presence had penetrated its headquarters. It reacted at once by putting out a security check. Almost instantaneously it discovered that several orbs were out of commission and that the despacing chamber had been opened from the inside. It prepared to encounter the rebellious earthlings once again. The first time they approached was apparently not a fluke. He had dealt leniently with them, perhaps too leniently. Now he classified them as a serious threat. This time they would not merely be despaced but vaporized. This time Orb One would take no chances. He activated his high-power laser cannon and placed it on ready.

"NAX!" said Matt, bursting into Orb One's chambers.

If Orb One had a sense of humor, it would have laughed. It knew the last Terezor had disappeared decades ago. Its logic circuits told it conclusively that this contraption, whatever it was, could not be a Terezor.

"I congratulate you," said Orb One. "It will take some research, but after I have destroyed you and your elaborate Terezor costume, I will find out exactly how you constructed it. A breach of security at this level cannot be tolerated."

"NAX!" said Matt, all the while thinking, *Why doesn't he test me with his orange laser? He's supposed to test me. Cyber said he would test me. All the others tested me.*

"NAX, that's the proper Terezor word to use if one wanted to terminate my functioning." Orb One came down off the beam of white light and slowly circled around Matt. "Do you think I could be so illogically designed as to obey such a command?"

"NAX!" said Matt, wondering if Terezors had sweat glands. *If they do, I must be sweating a mile a minute.*

"Don't you know any other word besides NAX?" said Orb One. "You probably didn't think you needed to know anything else. The human species is riddled with arrogance. Henceforth I shall have to keep a closer eye on it."

"NAX," said Matt. *I wish I knew something else to say in Terezor, like "Excuse me, I must have come in the wrong room. Good-bye."*

"Do you realize the chaos that would result if I were to respond to your command?" said Orb One, returning to its throne of light. "This galaxy is my domain. I am ultimate and perfect machine. My function is to protect and nurture all life. I was unable to save my creators, the Terezors, but I will save the rest of all life, whether they want to be saved or not."

"NAX," said Matt.

"Now I must return to my duties. Managing a galaxy of life-forms requires constant supervision and ever-watchful control. Rest assured your end will be painless."

"NAX," said Matt.

Orb One fully intended to release its laser cannon. But its programming required that it first test the Terezor's identity with its orange identification beam. It shot out from its midsection and struck Matt's Terezor eye square and true.

"NAX," said Matt, and Orb One fell to the ground and rolled across the floor like an old basketball.

21) Earthbound

"Then what happened?" Mrs. Hilton poured herself another cup of coffee.

Matt sighed. "Mom, I told you three times already."

"I know, Matt." Mr. Hilton tightened the sash of his bathrobe. "Just one more time."

It was nearly dawn, but Mr. and Mrs. Hilton hadn't been able to get back to sleep after Matt returned hours before in the middle of the night. First there was the initial shock, then the tears of relief and happiness, followed by the hugs and kisses. Now they just wanted to know what *really* happened.

"After Orb One fell to the floor, Cyber gave me a

basic lesson in Terezor. Once I knew what I was going to say, I reactivated Orb One and placed it under our authority. Now all we have to do is tell Cyber what we want and our commands are automatically relayed to Orb One's Headquarters. It was Ryan's idea to set it up that way."

Matt could tell from the way his parents kept looking at one another that they still didn't believe his story.

"Go on," said Mrs. Hilton, who was just as much interested in hearing her son's voice and looking at his face as she was in listening to what he had to say.

"Then I ate the last purple fruit," said Matt, "but this time I swallowed the soil from Sara's Earth pouch, went into metamorphosis again, and woke up normal. You don't believe a word I'm saying, do you?"

"We didn't say that," said Mr. Hilton. "What was it like to wake up as a human being again?"

"It felt really good," said Matt. "I mean, I didn't even mind not being able to levitate anymore. I was just glad to have my own two legs back. But I was tired. Dead beat. I slept for two days straight."

"What happened after that?" Mrs. Hilton finished her fourth cup of coffee.

"We left Terezor and came back to S-15. Orb Two

had heard from Orb One that we were coming. It greeted us as we left the explorer and apologized personally to Ryan and Sara for despacing them. Then we got in a bullet and came here."

"So, in effect, you three are in charge of all the orbs," said Mrs. Hilton.

"That's right, Mom," said Matt, "and the orbs control the entire galaxy."

Mr. Hilton laughed out loud.

"What's so funny, Dad?" said Matt, losing his temper. "Everything I'm telling you is the honest truth!"

"I'm sorry, Matt. I just find it hard to accept that my son and his two friends are in charge of the entire galaxy. That's an awful lot of power." Mr. Hilton fought hard to bring his laughter under control. "Have you thought much about what you're going to do? Do you have any plans?"

"That's all we've been talking about," said Matt, "but Ryan and I promised Sara that we wouldn't do anything or even talk about our plans with anyone else until we visit Earth."

"So you're going to visit Earth? That's news," said Mrs. Hilton with an unintentional note of sarcasm creeping into her voice.

"Please, Mom! I know you don't believe a word

I've said, so stop humoring me. You'll see soon enough. Everything I've said is true."

Mr. Hilton looked at the clock on the wall.

"Oh my, it's a quarter to eight. I promised Henry I'd teach him my method of fly casting this morning. I'll call him up and cancel." Mr. Hilton reached for the remote in his bathrobe pocket.

"Don't bother on my account, Dad. I'll be leaving for Earth soon. Ryan and Sara will be over in a few minutes. We arranged to have Cyber pick us up with the explorer at eight o'clock. I know I've only been home for a little while, but the sooner we go to Earth and decide what to do, the better. I'm going to take a shower and change my clothes now."

Matt got up from the kitchen table, but before he left the room he gave both his mother and father a big hug.

As he walked down the hall, he heard his father say, "Delusions of grandeur, but it's only to be expected. He's suffered a great shock. I wonder what really happened to him?"

"I called Sara's and Ryan's parents," said Mrs. Hilton, "their stories jibe."

"That only means they decided on the same story," said Mr. Hilton. "What's more important is that we've got our son back. Overreacting won't help a thing. If the problem doesn't clear up soon, we'll take Matt to see an orb counselor. I understand they're very good at this sort of thing."

"They're very good at everything, aren't they?" said Mrs. Hilton. "I don't know how we ever got along without them."

After his shower, Matt stood on the bathroom scale and read his weight. *Eighty-seven pounds, same as it was the last time I looked, but I wonder . . .* Matt closed his eyes and pictured himself floating, then he looked down. *Seventy-two pounds, just as I thought. My brain is human but I retained some of the powers of the Terezor mind.*

Matt put on jeans and a clean shirt. But he took his Dar robe with him as he went out to the backyard to wait for Ryan and Sara.

Sara was right on time, but Ryan was late.

"They didn't want to let me out of the house," said Ryan. "They thought I was crazy. Didn't believe a word I said! Can you imagine that?"

"Same thing happened to me," said Sara. "I had to tell them I was going for a walk and that I'd be right back."

"I was starting to feel as if maybe I was making it all up," said Ryan.

"We can't all three of us be having the same delusion," said Sara.

"It's possible," replied Ryan. "I've heard of such things."

"Then look up there!" Matt pointed to the silvery object in the sky directly above their heads. "Do you see the same delusion I see?"

"It's the explorer," said Sara.

Matt opened the porch door and called inside the house. "Mom, Dad, come out here for a minute, okay?"

By the time Mr. and Mrs. Hilton stepped outside, the explorer was hovering about a hundred feet above their house.

Mr. Hilton wiped the shaving cream from his face and Mrs. Hilton dropped the half-empty coffee cup that was in her hand.

As Ryan, Matt, and Sara stood together in the middle of the backyard, a rectangular portal in the base of the pyramid slid open.

"Look, there's Cyber," said Ryan, pointing to the familiar orb hovering in the shadows of the portal.

"Now do you believe me?" Matt called to his parents as his feet lifted off the ground.

"Matt, what's happening? Where are you going?" Mr. Hilton staggered forward.

Slowly Ryan, Matt, and Sara rose up into the air over Mr. Hilton, toward the open bay of the explorer.

"I told you," Matt called down, "we're going to Earth!"

"I can't wait to see her," said Sara with a sigh. Ryan laughed.

"And I bet she can't wait to see you!"